Suddenly António's playing a flute and the music runs a silver river along my spine and through my chest. Helena's leaning back against the couch. Susana's sitting close to me, rocking back and forth, her long legs stretched out in front of her, her wide feet now bare. The pleasure in me is so strong that the two languages converge and with these new friends I feel the joining of my Portuguese and American self. This is too intense. I stand up and find my way to the kitchen and drink a large glass of cold water and then refill the glass, holding its slight chill against my forehead. I lean against the sink and feel goodness pumping through my body in a warm rush.

"Are you all right?" Helena asks.

"Oh, yes." I set down the glass and turn towards her.

"You're crying."

"It's only because I feel so good. I feel so good," I say. "I wish I could tell you."

Helena wraps her arms around me in one full sweep, the full length of our bodies finally touching each other . . .

About the Author

Sue Gambill was born in 1951 in Eastern Kentucky and was raised outside of Cincinnati, Ohio. During the first fifteen years of her adult life she moved from town to town with great frequency, but is now pleased to be setting down roots in Tallahassee, Florida.

Heartscape

by
Sue Gambill

The Naiad Press, Inc.
1989

Printed in the United States of America
First Edition

Cover design by Pat Tong and Bonnie Liss
    (Phoenix Graphics)
Typeset by Sandi Stancil

Library of Congress Cataloging-in-Publication Data

Gambill, Sue, 1951—
    Heartscape.

    I. Title.
PS3557.A447H4 1989   813.54   88-29121
ISBN 0-941483-33-9 (pbk.)

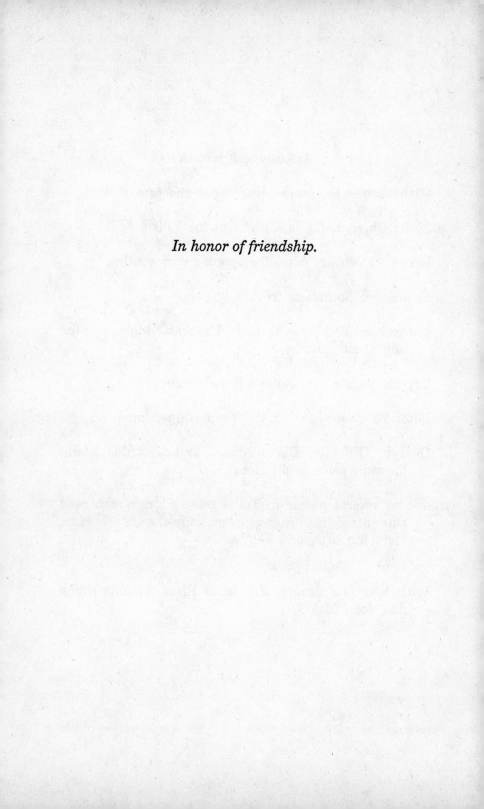

In honor of friendship.

Acknowledgments

With thanks to: Anna Alvarez, for the fun of it;

Leslie Clayton, for late night phone calls;

Rachel Guido de Vries, for spontaneous continuity;

Felicia, for boundless friendship;

Katherine V. Forrest and Deborah Malmud, for important lessons;

Crystal Wakoa, for our work of harmony;

Mimi Wilkinson, for all the right connections;

Georgia O'Keeffe, Diane Arbus, and Gertrude Stein, for wonderful inspiration;

and to several people in Tallahassee, Florida who read this novel in progress, especially Laura Newton, Heidi Roberts, and Felicia.

With love and deep gratitude to Elisa Outeiro Braga and João Melo.

Prologue

For years I've made my trips to airports rather frantic productions. Whether flying in or out of Cincinnati, Boston, Atlanta or Portland there has always been a last minute rush of finding someone to drive me, followed by a long run down some corridor with my suitcase in tow. New York's Kennedy International is the only airport where I arrive at least an hour before flight time. I like to sit and watch the crowds of people. Some walk by with eyes wide with astonishment, others with stunned, sagging jaws. The colors and patterns of their shirts and dresses are banners of the countries of their births, their various languages are a sweet melody to my ears.

My trips across the ocean began in 1973 when I decided at the last minute to attend an international women's conference in Portugal. The plan was to gather new ideas for the rural health project I was involved with in eastern Indiana. I was fascinated by the enormous variety of women at the conference — their languages and accents, the clothes they wore, the work they were doing. I was twenty-one years old and had never been outside of the Midwestern United States. I hadn't realized until then how very hungry I was for diversity. The best idea I brought back from that conference was to pack my bags and return to Portugal to live. I thought it might be forever.

Two years later my father died and I found myself walking down the long ramp of the Cincinnati terminal, my family gathered anxiously at the far end, held there by a metal detector through which I would have to walk into their open arms.

If you ask my family about that return they will tell you that for the first three months I spoke English with a heavy foreign accent and it made my small nieces cry. It's one of the many stories told when my Mom, my brothers and sisters, their children, and I sit around a big meal at the kitchen table. That's where all our stories are told. But of that particular time I don't remember much. There are pictures of me then and in all of them I have a vacant, lost look in my eyes. The first four months are still a blank in my memory.

I don't know why I didn't immediately return to Portugal. The shock of my cultural transition back

2

into the United States was more than a temporary adjustment. For the next three years my night dreams were filled with desperate attempts to return across the ocean. I did return for a few short visits with my friends Joana and Miguel, but each time I came back to the States. I don't know why. What I do know is my history, the past ten years of repeatedly packing up my belongings and traveling about the U.S. in search of some place to call home. I've lived on the East Coast and the West, in the South, and even back in the Midwest. I'm thirty-four years old and tired of moving.

It's October, 1985 and I'm sitting in Kennedy International. Some friends wanted to drive me down from Provincetown, but I told them I needed to make this trip alone. Nobody else knows this, but maybe this time I'm going for good.

1

My seat is right between two worlds. On my left
is a young North American, a jet-set blonde whose
feathered hair accentuates the make-up blush of her
cheeks and the hazy blue accent of shadow above her
light blue eyes. She says she's off for a fun-filled two
weeks in Morocco where she'll join a male companion
flying in from Cairo. They meet in different places
around the globe at least two or three times a year.
On my right is a Portuguese man whose solemn face
is capped by a well-worn black beret. The deep lines
along his leathery olive skin map a lineage to some

5

farming or fishing village. While the plane taxies into position the man turns and speaks Portuguese with a woman and two children sitting several rows back. I close my eyes and say a quick blessing for a safe flight while the plane builds momentum down the long runway. I rush with excitement as we race towards the friends and country that for so long have filled my dreams. The massive craft lifts its wheels from the concrete and I pull further and further away from the confusion and struggles I feel.

As soon as the plane levels off many of the Portuguese men get out of their seats, leaving the women and children behind. They wander up and down the aisles to converse loudly with other passengers, their excited hands punctuating the air. Each man is dressed in the somber colors of village people — dark brown, blue or black. Each man wears a beret that declares his Latin spirit.

The blonde says, "God, they all seem to know each other."

"They probably don't, but what they share are saudades, a sweet and melancholy yearning for their homeland," I explain.

It makes me remember the fishermen in Provincetown, many of them third generation, who've never seen Portugal yet have inherited this passionate yearning. Finally I work up the courage to use my rusty Portuguese. I speak to the man sitting next to me and his face opens in great animation as he speaks hungrily of the land he hasn't seen in three years.

For hours I listen to the excitement in the conversation around me as the emigrants trace their histories back to the Alentejo, the Douro River,

Trás-os-Montes. The flight attendants enter into the joyful mood, exchanging stories and laughter with the passengers as they walk up and down the aisles.

Eventually the cabin calms down as people drift into sleep. I welcome the quiet, but also miss the entertaining stories that kept me from thinking about my life in the States and about Sarah's recent challenge. Sarah's a good friend, but she hasn't understood any of my choices this past year — my involvement with Deirdre, my move from the Catskills to Provincetown, my quitting the peace coalition work, and now this trip to Portugal. I told her I just need a break but she won't accept that. She says I'm running away. I say I need some distance between me and the States.

The Portuguese man next to me snores lightly as his head slumps onto his chest. I wish I could get up and walk around but his legs block passage to the aisle. I turn my mind to Portugal and think about my friends Joana and Miguel, their three teenage children, and the friends and colleagues who pass through their three-story house with its high ceilings, its modern paintings and antique furniture inherited from a long family lineage. It is with these friends I share a bond that has lasted longer than any American friendship.

I reach into my handbag and pull out a book of Diane Arbus photographs, my present to Joana and Miguel. They like to challenge and expand their traditional heritage, so I'm sure they'll find her bizarre perspective interesting. I flip through the pages and return to the introduction, hoping that reading will calm my excitement and allow me to sleep. It's hard to focus on the words printed on the page, but still I hold the book, close my eyes, and think about our flight through this enormous dark night sky.

I drift in and out of a light sleep, until I fully wake to the smell of coffee, my neck stiff with a dull ache. I stumble to the bathroom. The mirror reflects in great detail the light pattern of wrinkles that have begun to gather around my eyes during the past year. I run my hands through my curly hair and shake my head to dispel the final edges of sleep. During my last visit my hair had been short and straight, my skin pale white. Now I sport a new perm in my sun-bleached hair and a Cape Cod summer tan. I lean close to the mirror and grin. I wish I could brush my teeth.

Back in my seat I watch morning dawn along the horizon as we begin the descent towards that stretch of land on the eastern side of the Atlantic. I'm crossing light years inside myself and the thrill is ice cold and fire along the underside of my skin. I now sit completely silent between the dozing American woman and the elated Portuguese man, my own worlds careening about inside me.

As the plane touches the runway the Portuguese passengers greet their native country with uproarious applause. They jump out of their seats and begin pulling down overhead luggage while the flight attendant frantically pleads with them in English to wait until the plane has come to a complete stop.

Outside the airport I grab a taxi. We speed along streets, precariously dodging cars, swerving around corners, and halting with a sudden jolt at every red light. The driver, discovering my knowledge of Portuguese, immediately begins a heated monologue about the bad economy, listing with a great flourish all of his complaints and struggles. I get in an occasional nod of agreement, amazed how this language I haven't spoken in four years clicks on again inside my brain.

This section is mostly industrial. The long stretches of gray buildings with few windows, large metal doors, and huge cement docks look like the industrial area of any major city in North America. The differences are the European drivers, cobblestone streets, and dark haired Portuguese people who walk the sidewalks with a sullen expression on their faces, an intriguing contrast to the passionate emotions just below the surface.

When we pull up to the next light the driver yells out playfully to some people on the corner, "Olha, esta senhora é Americana e ela fala Português."

A woman steps out into the street, away from the cluster of people. Her arms are wrapped around a skinny teenage boy whom she seems to lift and carry along beside her wide hips. His arms and legs move spasmodically. The woman wraps her hand into the boy's gnarled hand and extends both towards the car window. Her eyes capture my eyes with a pleading, insistent gaze.

"Dá-mim dinheiro, menina." Give me money.

Just then the light turns green and we jolt forward, leaving a silvery chill along my skin, a vivid image not from the book of Diane Arbus, but people an arm's length away.

The street outside the train station is filled with large black and green taxis, old cars, trucks and buses, and people everywhere carrying bags, including village women with huge baskets balanced on their heads. My train car is divided into compartments that seat six and I enter the first one, closing the heavy sliding door behind me. I choose a seat by the window and watch people walking and running in various directions outside the train. Inside, passengers push by my door lugging bags and packages, but no one enters my compartment. By the time the train sends out a high-pitched whistle and lurches forward with a clatter of metal, I still have the space all to myself.

We pass through the outskirts of Lisbon. Rows of modern apartments give way to a large haphazard section of barracas, low shacks made of scavenged wood and tin. These are followed by small green fields with boundaries marked by lines of evergreens and eucalyptus or skinny streams of water with banks of tall grasses. Occasionally we pass buildings of whitewashed walls and orange tiled roofs and men in village black working among the fields with oxen, or women walking along small paths with ceramic jugs balanced upon their heads. Along one river I glimpse women scrubbing clothes against large rocks. The light green fields and clusters of dark green trees are a welcome contrast to the wide stretch of gray horizon I left behind in Provincetown.

The clacking of the train, the gentle rocking, and the bright light of morning make my tired, aching eyes heavy. I want to stretch out on the empty seat. Knowing this would insult passengers who'll board further down the line, I pull a sweatshirt out of my backpack and roll it into a makeshift pillow against the window and immediately fall into an exhausted sleep.

Later when I wake the five other seats in the

compartment are filled. Across from me sits a village woman in a dark print shirtwaist dress, a black scarf on her head. From a cloth bag at her feet she pulls out a hand-size loaf of bread which she hands to the small boy sitting next to her. On the other side of the boy sits a man in a loose-fitting suit and a black fedora. He puffs on a cigarette that fills the cabin with an acrid, throat-burning smell. Next to me sit two women, both in plaid woolen skirts and pastel sweaters. They talk about their classes at the university.

I excuse myself and go into the corridor where I lean next to an open window and let the rush of temperate air run across my face, blowing my hair back away from my shoulders. I watch the small green and brown hills rise and fall and rise again. More people come out into the corridor and group around the windows. The man standing next to me says Coimbra is the next station.

With great excitement I step inside the compartment and pull down my handbag, suitcase, and backpack, trying not to bang against anyone. Returning to the open window I watch the changing terrain for another half hour, anticipation spreading along my skin in goose bumps and a rising electric charge inside my chest.

As we make the last long curve and pull into Coimbra I look out at the large crowd gathered between the station and the edge of the long cement platform. Those people nearest the edge almost touch the passing cars as the brakes slowly bring the massive train to a hissing halt.

The corridor is packed with people loaded down with bags. I inch along the corridor behind an old

11

man hunched over a cane. When I reach the doorway I hear my name called out once, then twice, but can't locate the caller. I head in the direction of the voice, gradually making a path through people who are pushing every which way.

Isabel is the first to reach me. "Olá, Leslie," she shouts. Inches taller than when I'd last seen her, she grabs me around the waist and gives a big hug. Her height as a sixteen-year-old is now nearly equal to mine.

"Olham aos cabelos dela!" Look at her hair, Joana says. She wraps her arms around Isabel and me and pulls us against her chest. Isabel laughs as my curls tickle her cheek.

The three of us pull apart and Miguel leans past Isabel and says in proud English, "Welcome Leslie. I hope you've had a good trip." Smelling of fresh aftershave he places his cheek against mine, and kisses the side of my face.

"Olá Miguel."

"Bem-vindo," Zé says. Now a tall, skinny thirteen-year-old, he waves shyly from where he stands behind Cristina.

Cristina smiles and says softly, "Bem-vindo, Leslie."

They ask me how the trip was.

"Good," I say, "but very tiring."

"You can take a nap before lunch," Joana says, wrapping her arm into mine and turning us towards the parking lot. I feel a sure rush of pleasure as I stand among my friends, a family not of blood relations but one chosen in kindred spirit.

Zé starts off in front of us with my suitcase. His dark hair is buzzed on the sides, and with the longer wavy top his style seems almost punkish. He's dressed in a soccer T-shirt, impeccably pressed blue jeans, and slightly scruffy sneakers.

Isabel skips up beside us with my backpack in tow. Her hair is a bushy shoulder-length cut, more styled than I last remember. Her face is highlighted with a natural blush. She's wearing flowered pedal pushers, a bright yellow blouse, and canvas shoes.

"Everyone's coming over this afternoon to see you," she says excitedly, her face very close to mine.

"We're going to see whose names you've forgotten," Zé says back over his shoulder.

"Plus, there'll be some people you don't yet know," Joana adds, catching me with her familiar dark warm eyes.

Zé and Isabel have changed since my last visit, moving from childhood into adolescence. But it's Cristina, in her first year at the university, who seems different. She's wearing a dark blue pleated skirt with a blue and green checkered blouse. Her hair is pulled back in a bun that gives her face a sharp, angular look, and her comfortable penny loafers have been replaced by dark blue pumps. Her walk is stiff, her steps short and very controlled.

Miguel groans as he heaves my suitcase into the trunk. I throw in my backpack and handbag. The three teenagers and myself crowd into the back seat of the car. From the passenger side of the front seat Joana smiles back at us in our cramped quarters. "Leslie, you've known my babies since they were small. Now they're nearly grown and ready to begin their own families."

"Don't rush us," Isabel says.

We speed through the skinny streets, making

13

sharp turns and quick stops. Miguel calls out after other drivers, while Zé and Isabel pump me with questions about the latest in American rock and roll. Their teenage curiosity reveals my own ignorance as I don't recognize the names of most of the bands they mention.

Miguel jumps in between the questions with descriptions of the Italian opera he and Joana attended in Rome last August.

"No pai! We don't want to hear about it again!" Isabel says, grinning in my direction.

"Oh pai, don't make us listen," Zé says.

Joana and I laugh. Cristina sits quietly, except for an occasional groan and a slap to her brother's shoulders as he shifts in her lap.

At the house I unpack presents: bound sketch pads and the photo book for Joana and Miguel, comic books to help Zé with his English, a wild variety of stationary for Isabel who has several pen pals, and perfume for Cristina.

Isabel and I drag my suitcase and backpack to the bedroom that will be mine during this visit. Isabel points to the large collection of postcards on one wall. "These are from my pen pals. Here are a couple you sent me," she says. She points to a beach scene with Cape Cod printed in big letters underneath. Next to that are photos of the Oregon coastline and the Smoky Mountains.

"Great collection," I say, looking across the wall at the other cards, including European, Asian, and African scenes.

"The writing's good practice for my English and French classes," she says. "Do you want to see pictures of the people I write to?" She jumps over to a drawer and flings it open.

"I'd love to," I say, as Joana and Zé enter the doorway, "but maybe not right this minute."

"Let her freshen up first," Joana says.

I tug at Isabel's bright, flowered pedal pushers. "Since you're so good at clothes, Isabel, will you pick out something for me to wear when I get out of the shower?"

"Sure," she says, eagerly putting my suitcase on the bed.

With the water on full force I let it beat against my neck and down across my shoulders, loosening my tightened muscles. I soap my skin with a fat bar of minty soap and watch the bubbles wash away as I turn my chest and belly into the water, remembering that it was water that bonded my friendship with Joana.

When we first knew each other Zé was a tiny one-year-old with a nearly bald head. We went to the shore for a week, and as usual Joana and I took the kids to the beach for the afternoon. While Joana and I discussed Fellini and Bergman films Cristina and Isabel took toddling Zé across the sand. They wandered too close to the water and Zé was swept off his feet by a wave and pulled out a short distance by a quick undertow. It only took a minute or two for me to cross the sand, splash through the shifting water, but longer to locate and pull him out of the tumbling waves. Already his skin had a tinge of blue. I stood up with him wrapped in my arms, and put his little mouth to mine as the cold water moved around my legs. Joana stood frozen to the edge of our blanket, screaming a loud piercing sound.

15

That was a moment when history hung suspended, the path from water to blanket an endless stretch of slow, steady breaths that first brought back color and then a coughing little baby who stirred in his mother's arms. She cried and rocked him for an hour, her body in a violent tremor until he nestled against her breast and slept. Then she lay with him on the blanket, curled around his body, and moved with him into a deep sleep.

Later, when Miguel heard the story, he said he was greatly indebted and praised me highly. Joana and I never spoke of it again, but the water that nearly killed her son became instead a deep passage between our hearts, a bond that felt as close as birth itself.

I step out of the shower, dry off, and put on Isabel's robe. In the bedroom Zé and Isabel have laid my clothes out on the bed and across the table and are asking Joana's advice in picking out a blouse. I push aside some of the clothes and make a small space for myself on the bed. I say to Isabel, "Pick out something for yourself to wear." Before she's made a decision I slide swiftly into a deep sleep.

* * * * *

Cristina taps on the door and calls me for lunch. I wake out of English into Portuguese, still groggy with this transition.

Everyone is in the dining room, standing around like restless birds. When I join them Joana takes her seat and everyone follows suit. I take the seat pointed out to me, between Zé in my flamingo top and Isabel in my Zora Neale Hurston sweatshirt. I arise a

16

second later when Constança, the housekeeper, comes into the room with two bowls of steaming soup. She had been out shopping when I arrived earlier.

"Olá, Constança!" I say enthusiastically. She puts down the soup and we quickly place light kisses on each cheek.

"Boa tarde, menina," she responds in her traditionally sedate manner, but with a big smile. She looks the same as always in a plain shirtwaist dress and a white kitchen apron, her hair pulled back and tied at the nape of her neck and hands clasped at her waist as if waiting for instruction.

Conversation continues over the table as Constança takes out the empty soup bowls and brings in a big plate of fish and rice. Miguel immediately takes the large serving platter and with great fanfare passes it to my end of the table. We all respond with smiles.

Every visit we relive this tradition. Twelve years ago when I came into their home to teach conversational English, I was immediately adopted into this family that loves to absorb the world's great diversity. That evening Constança prepared a similar large platter of fish, and Miguel passed to me the honor of serving. Having been brought up on frozen fish sticks in the Midwest, I had no concept of bones. I sawed crosswise at the fish until Miguel rescued me. It was at that moment we began the exciting explorations of our different cultures. Now I expertly lift away the bone and serve large pieces of the white fish.

After lunch Miguel, Joana and I settle into the large couch and the fat living room chairs, easing out of our initial jittery excitement. Constança brings

17

small cups of espresso and my favorite pineapple cake.

Joana begins talking as if the past four years have been only a slight interruption from an earlier conversation, a continuing dialogue that now spans more than a decade. The only visible differences to this familiarity are the new gray streaks that run through Joana's thick short black hair and a settling plumpness in her forty-year-old, unexercised body. It's Miguel, at forty-six, who more drastically shows the changes. His Bohemian goatee is long since shaven and his cropped black hair now recedes in two half moons back along his temples. His paunch is large and strains against the waistline of his pants. He has a tired look in his eyes.

"I want to know about all of my questions," Joana says, "you know, the ones you neglected to answer this past year." Her direct gaze tells me avoidance is out of the question.

"I couldn't explain things very well through a letter," I say.

"Since you moved out of New York last year your letters have had a different tone. You seem distracted, flustered."

I thought I'd done so well at hiding my feelings, but even with an ocean between us Joana knew something was going on. I felt myself running inside, not wanting to talk about this now.

"It's been over a year since you told us about any projects," Miguel says.

"I needed a break," I explain, "so I dropped out for a while."

"That doesn't sound like you," Joana says. "You've always been involved with other people."

18

"Remember when I spent time in jail for climbing a fence at a weapons facility?" I say. "It felt good that day with a crowd cheering us on. It was even good in jail. I mean, there was a connection, a feeling of doing something important. Two weeks later I walked outside into an empty parking lot and watched a caravan of military jeeps drive past on the road. When I turned back towards the prison I could see the hands of the few remaining women waving at me from an open window. It just seemed futile. All of those years of marching and writing letters and nothing had changed. Something just broke in me. I moved to Provincetown where all I had to think about was the ocean and earning enough money to make it through the winter." My voice begins to catch in my throat and I stop talking in order to hold back the tears.

"But that's not enough for you, is it?" Joana says.

"No, and that's why I'm here, to get some sense of direction."

Miguel laughs. "This may not be the place. The economy is a mess and arranging employment could be difficult."

"That's not why she came," Joana says defensively.

"Well, it's true that getting a job isn't easy and she could take work away from a Portuguese."

"Miguel! We'll figure it out. She can stay with us as long as she wants."

"I'm just speaking realistically," Miguel says. "Of course, Leslie, you can stay as long as you need to. It's just that Portugal may not be the answer you're looking for."

Joana shoots a quick look at Miguel and I wonder if there's more here than his practical concerns. Maybe this wasn't the right time to come. A tiny fear flickers in my stomach but I push it away, thinking if it weren't for this country and these friends where else could I turn?

"When you're in the States, Leslie, I have so many conversations in my head with you," Joana says. "I've really missed you and I'm glad you're here. I want you to make yourself at home and take the time that's necessary, because I know you'll find what you need. I want you to come to school and see what my students are doing and I can't wait to show you the studio where I paint. I've been so productive since your last visit." She nods towards the new canvases I see around the room and begins to explain her recent rediscovery of color.

Joana's eyes light with excitement as she talks about her work. I breathe easier having told them about dropping out of things in New York. They don't seem shocked or disappointed or overly concerned. I know Joana and I eventually will discuss it all in great detail.

I watch Miguel watching her, her hands like a dance gracing each sentence, his love evident in the way his body leans into her words. I sometimes wonder if he feels jealous about the friendship Joana and I share. The last visit, when I told Joana I was a lesbian it didn't surprise her. She said she had a feeling about it because of the intensity of our friendship. I didn't tell Miguel then because I didn't want to deal with his reaction. Joana said she probably wouldn't tell him either. But now, if I decide to make this country my home, I want to come out

20

to him. I look at the photograph hanging behind the chair where Miguel is sitting. It's from the first year we met. The children are all small. Joana, Miguel and I have faces that seem much younger than I remember.

Joana asks if I'm feeling tired and want to rest again before people arrive. I guess the slight strain of the language is beginning to show on my face. Before I can answer the doorbell rings and the kids come downstairs to answer it. I can hear Miguel's brother Paulo, his wife Teresa, and their children laughing and talking in the foyer. Miguel goes to greet them, and Joana leans across the couch and places a light kiss on my cheek.

"I'm happy you're here," she says.

"We have so much to talk about, and now that I'm here we have the time," I say with a big smile as the others enter the living room.

I stand up to greet Paulo and Teresa, while their four children gather around. "Teresa, you're pregnant again," I say, patting her large belly as we lean to kiss cheeks.

"Didn't I tell you?" Joana asks.

"No, you didn't. And, Paulo, what is this?" I ask jokingly.

Paulo grabs the well combed and curled tips of his long mustache and gives them an extra twirl, his role as a jester confirmed by this new trademark. "Do you like it?" he asks. "I had quite a battle with the director. He was convinced it would make my students absolutely wild."

"It would be nice," Miguel says, "to have a mustache to blame that on!"

"Where is this new baby I haven't yet met?" I

bend to lift the tiny boy. "Whenever I come here there are more little Portuguese!"

"That's because Portuguese men know how to make babies," Paulo says. He gives a hearty laugh, looks around for agreement, and then reaches out to wrap me and his young son in a big hug. The doorbell rings again and the kids run to answer it.

Soon all of Miguel and Joana's brothers and sisters have arrived for Sunday tea to welcome me back again, along with a couple of Joana's colleagues from school and several friends who are painters and photographers. Some people I recognize only by sight, others I've known for years. After wandering about among the various groups I join Joana on the couch. She and several women are discussing children. Joana smiles at me and pats my thigh. I sip warm tea and feel the familiar pleasure of belonging. As I listen to the women I drift in and out of Portuguese, listening more to the music of the language than its meaning.

I hear the doorbell and Miguel goes to answer it. A moment later Miguel steps out of the foyer with a woman who catches my interest. I've never see her before. Paulo joins them and the woman leans back against the wall. The two men stand in front of her, partially blocking my view. I glimpse an impish grin on her face as she leans forward to nudge Paulo. She winks at Miguel and both men laugh. Paulo takes a step sideways as he leans his head back laughing, and I get a full view. She stands out in this crowd of dark-haired people because of her light auburn hair that tends more towards red than brown. It's thick and frizzy and ends just at her collar. She's dressed in a satiny green blouse with long puffy sleeves, baggy pants with burnt orange and white vertical stripes, and bright yellow shoes. She's definitely the most colorful person in the room. She's either a foreigner or very original, or maybe there have been style changes since my last visit.

Suddenly she looks past the men and seems to meet my gaze. The edges of her mouth turn up slightly and I blush and turn away. When I look back she's talking again, her attentive eyes focused on Miguel, a hand gesturing in midair.

"Who is that woman?" I ask, leaning close to Joana.

"That's Helena. Didn't you meet her when you were here before?"

"I would have remembered."

"She and I must have become friends just after your last visit," Joana says. "She's an artist, the one with the studio where I sometimes paint. I haven't written you about her?"

"No."

"I can't imagine why I haven't. She and I do so much together and I've told her all about you. Come on," she says, taking my hand, "I feel like the two of you already know each other."

Joana walks me over to Miguel, Paulo and Helena. She kisses Helena and then the whole group turns in my direction as Joana introduces me.

"It's a pleasure to meet you, Leslie," Helena says, her voice deep and comfortable. "I've heard so much about you."

"It's my pleasure," I say as we take each other's hand, hers large and warm with a firm grip. I feel shy and uncertain what to say next. I listen for a few minutes to the others talk about an art exhibit and then excuse myself.

23

In the kitchen Constança offers to make me a cup of warm milk and retrieves a couple of small meat pastries from the spread on the dining room table. She closes the kitchen door when I explain that I'm needing a break from the crowd. Jet lag is starting to catch me, but hopefully the protein will give me a second lift.

After eating I find Helena sitting on the stairway outside the kitchen door. "Want to go outside?" she asks, motioning up the stairs towards the balcony off the living room. "We can speak English if you like, or maybe you'd prefer to be alone."

"It would be nice to talk with you," I say, extending my hand to help her to her feet. "But let's speak Portuguese. I can handle one person, it's the large groups that take me awhile to adjust to."

"I used to live in England," Helena says as she stops at the dining room table and picks up a napkin and two of the sweet pastries. "I know what it's like to readapt to a language you haven't spoken in a while."

"There's such an incentive with Portuguese," I say, "because it's so melodious."

"You speak it very well," Helena says.

"Well, I'm not always so great on the verbs and I might need to ask you for a word or two."

"No problem," she says, as we walk up the steps and out onto the balcony.

Helena places the pastry on a table top near a couple of bird cages. We watch the fluttering finches and then look at each other awkwardly for a moment. She has a pretty face, olive brown skin and chestnut brown eyes.

"Have you ever been to New Mexico where Georgia O'Keeffe paints?" she asks.

"No, I haven't," I say. "You're familiar with her work?"

"Yes, she's my favorite of the American painters. Among writers I enjoy Gertrude Stein. I've been to her residence in Paris. It's marvelous to walk the streets where writers and artists lived at the turn of the century and to imagine what their lives were like."

"Maybe someday people will walk this street," I say, leaning against the intricate iron latticework of the balcony and pointing to the street below. "They'll say here is where the famous artists of the 1980s gathered for their afternoon parties.

"Wouldn't that be lovely," Helena says. She offers me one of the apple pastries and then takes one herself. "I often wonder if their lives were like ours or if they were different in some way." She leans back against the railing, the open collar of her blouse revealing several strands of gold chain.

"Do you mean was it more exotic for them?" I take a bite of the apple sweet and enjoy the taste and smell of cinnamon.

"Yes, maybe that is the question," Helena says.

I turn and look back through the large sliding glass doors into the living room where people mingle among the antique furniture and the modern paintings and photographs. "There's a timelessness to such gatherings," I say, indicating the room of people in casual, modern dress. "We talk politics and philosophy, and some of you create art. That's a leisure some would call exotic."

"And others would call necessary," Helena says.

We turn away from the glass doors and look out over the town. Across the street is a high, thick stone wall whose cracked and chipped whitewash is covered with posters of political parties, whose symbols are large, bold visual images and easily recognizable: Social Democrats, Socialists, United Party Alliance, and Communists. In smaller print each poster carries its promise for a better Portugal. From the balcony I can see over the wall into several skinny alleys lined with long row houses where large families live in one or two rooms. Ropes filled with freshly washed clothes stretch out in a crisscross pattern above the cobblestone walkways.

"If I lived there," I say, gesturing to the houses, "I imagine my experience of Portugal would be quite different."

"Or if you lived in a village," Helena says, placing one hand on my shoulder and pointing with the other out past the town.

I love this closeness that is so Portuguese. I already feel comfortable with Helena, her easy openness reminding me of Joana. "I sat next to an emigrant on the plane," I say, "and I've been wondering where he's sitting now, knowing how different his reality of Portugal is from mine."

"Maybe sometime you'd like to meet the people I work with in the villages," Helena says.

"What do you do?" I ask.

"I teach art in the middle school here in Coimbra. And, as Joana told you, I paint. You'll need to come and see my studio. Joana loves it there."

"She's told me about it."

"She's told me a lot about you," Helena says. "She really loves you."

"Her friendship is so important to me," I say. I meet Helena's brown eyes and we stand quietly for a long moment, unafraid of our direct gaze.

"Anyway," she says, breaking the stillness, "the other thing I do is work with people in the villages around Coimbra. We're organizing work cooperatives and figuring out some other projects."

"You're a busy woman."

"I don't believe in being bored!"

When Helena and I come back into the house the women and most of the kids have congregated in the living room and the men are downstairs around the computer. I sit on the floor by Joana's feet, lean an arm across her knees, and listen to the conversation.

Isabel, still wearing my Zora Neale Hurston sweatshirt, suddenly appears at the edge of the group. I watch her watching me, shifting back and forth on her feet as the conversation moves around the room. Then in a swift moment she says to me across the circle, "Leslie, how were you able to arrange your trip here so quickly?"

"Isabel," someone says sharply.

The sudden quieting of the women makes me know this is a question of wide interest. As I fumble about with my thoughts Joana leans forward in her chair, attentively awaiting my response.

"I'll tell you later," I say to Isabel, trying not to force a smile, knowing Joana will so easily read my face. In this quick moment she already understands that, for this visit, I need them to give me time to tell my stories.

2

I've been trying to speak Portuguese like English, with my lips barely moving. I have to remind myself to open wide for the Portuguese sounds. It's almost a frightening thing as I begin to enter more into the spoken rhythms and feel a tremendous shift, my American self sliding further into the background. I'm afraid of losing that self, while at the same time I warmly welcome the more Portuguese part of me that has been in hiding in the U.S. these past four years. Will I ever find a balance between them?

* * * * *

Every morning before going off to school, Isabel and Zé are at my bedroom door to wake me and to crowd onto my bed. Isabel talks about American clothes and usually pokes around the closet. When I say she's welcome to wear anything she grabs a shirt or a pair of pants she's been dying to wear. She says all her friends at school keep asking where they can buy clothes like these. She loves a slight touch of being different, the flavor of being a foreigner; someday she'll explore the world beyond her country.

Zé talks about one of the comic books I brought him and the possibilities of making lots of money in America. Eventually Joana comes and chases the kids off to school, I take a quick shower, and Joana and I have a late breakfast.

This morning it's Cristina who comes to the door for Zé and Isabel. The two of them leave for school and Cristina hangs out in the doorway, not saying anything. When I invite her in she asks if I can come one day to her English class at the university.

"Sure, I'd love to," I say.

"I'll let you know when," she says and backs out the door.

I miss the rambunctious Cristina I used to know, and I'm not certain how to handle her stuffy move into womanhood. She makes me see there are parts of myself that could never fully settle into this culture. For example, my assertive behavior, instead of being seen as a woman's strength, is often interpreted as merely an American eccentricity.

* * * * *

Miguel always leaves early for the hospital. Joana's teaching hours vary, often leaving us a morning or an afternoon together. With the part of the day that's my own I explore the streets of Coimbra.

I pass outdoor cafés filled with students clustered about small tables, immersed in exuberant conversation between quick gulps of espresso and cappuccino. I watch village women in traditional black dress walking in and out of the open market with large, heavy baskets balanced upon their heads and chickens trussed up under their arms. I'd forgotten how wonderful it is that one can stare and no one seems to mind.

The rough earthy texture of the cobblestone streets are an abrupt contrast to the slick pavement of American highways. Here ancient history is alive in the pavement, in the horse-drawn carts that still clatter across the stones, and in the thick stone walls of the churches that protect grotesque, larger-than-life statues of the Virgin Mary, a bloodied Jesus Christ, and a wide selection of saints.

Today I enter the open air market where rows of stands display green vegetables, oranges, flowers, and racks of meat. Vendors shout out prices and encouragement to the people crowded around everywhere. I walk slowly through each of the aisles, my eyes and ears like a video camera. At one stand a man thrusts a chicken in my direction, calling out, "Menina, menina, compra aqui este frango." I smile, shake my head, and move on through the crowd. Everywhere people are talking, negotiating, touching and poking at fruit, buying slabs of cheese, carting off a bundle of greens or a bag of small fresh loaves of bread.

At one end of the market is a large building where all the fish are sold. As I enter the cavernous doorway the strong smell smacks me in the face and fills my head and lungs. I have an urge to turn and run, but instead decide to cross the huge cement floor of the building for the opposite door. Everywhere women call out, "Peixe, peixe fresca." I watch their large hands, palms up, beckoning across the mounds of sleek gray-silver fish whose tails and heads and eyes are intact.

One woman in a black rubber apron, her fish laid out on a high mound of chipped ice, calls out to a woman standing next to me, "Senhora, olha ao meu peixe que saiu hoje do mar." With hands red and wet from work, the vendor reaches into the large pile of fish, pulls one out, and thrusts her fingers into the slit along its belly. She reaches across the pile to hold out to the buyer the spread of its fresh insides. I turn away quickly, my stomach raw and unsettled. I slosh across the wet cement floor, trying to avoid small scraps of white fish in the puddles of water. I want sudden escape from the sharp smell that fills my nostrils, surprised at my revulsion and my desire to not be exposed, like the fish, to this mundane daily intimacy.

Finally I succeed in crossing to the second cavernous doorway. The bright sun strikes my eyes and for a moment I'm blinded by this transition

* * * * *

Joana's family has a rambling, ancient house in

31

the country where she and her eight brothers and sisters were born. Since everyone now lives in Coimbra, the place is mostly used for long weekend vacations where the whole family comes for a wild tangle of cousins, aunts, uncles, and grandparents; an exhausting experience with lots of good food and great conversations.

Neither of Joana's parents nor any of her brothers or sisters have been there in a month, so Joana and I volunteer to make the trip. The house and property are maintained by an elderly village couple, and though most of the land is no longer cultivated, there is still a small vineyard to keep the large extended family in wine for the year. Since harvesting has just taken place we're going to see about the work that has been done.

Joana changes from slacks into a woolen skirt, a thin sweater with a white blouse underneath, and the tiny silver cross that had been her great grandmother's. I put on chinos, by black leather Reeboks, and a flower print sweater that reflects how my mother wishes I would always dress. It's a bit too femme for my taste, but good cover in the villages where being American and unmarried are enough peculiar attributes without also needing to explain my favorite worn blue jeans and Tina Turner sweatshirt.

In the middle of our drive over we stop the car for a leisurely walk in a large field surrounded by low smooth hills.

"I wake up still surprised that my children are nearly grown," Joana says.

"What do you enjoy most about them?" I ask.

"They keep me fascinated with their strong opinions."

"A natural inheritance from you and Miguel," I say.

Joana stops for a moment, puts her hands on her wide hips, and looks out towards the endless blue sky. She wraps her arms across her breasts and turns to me with that look of focused attention so familiar between us. "I'm concerned about their futures. Positions in the university are limited and jobs are scarce. There aren't many alternatives if one of them doesn't get into the university."

"I'll take them to the States with me," I say, "there's always something to do there."

"I wouldn't have the money for it," Joana says, "plus I couldn't bear them being that far away. A girl down the street moved to Canada with her husband and her family is heartbroken."

"Then I'll take all of you," I add, wanting to find an easy solution.

"I love when you're with me," Joana says. "You're always thinking of other possibilities, even if they're not always practical."

"I forget how small Portugal is. In the States, if nothing else, you can always move to a new location, get a new start."

"It's more difficult here," Joana says.

I look at Joana's face and notice for the first time a slight sag under her jaw and the deepening texture of wrinkles around her mouth and eyes. "Was this a bad time for me to come?" I ask.

Joana wraps her arm around my shoulder and pulls me close. "I want you here all the time. Will you stay?"

"I don't know," I say.

As we circle the large field and walk back towards

the car, we are greeted by a melodious chiming of tiny bells. A large herd of goats crests along one of the knolls and heads into the little valley. The animals spread their gentle ringing like a wave out along the grassland, a shepherd and his dog guiding from behind. I stand in the sun with Joana, a comfortable silence between us, feeling a great rise of pleasure.

After a leisurely drive through hilly green countryside we arrive at the family home in late afternoon. Maria Jesus, the shy housekeeper, greets us out back. She's carrying a picking of greens bundled in a white apron tied around her waist.

"Boa tarde, Dona Joana. My husband has just gone to the fields," she says, indicating the direction with a turn of her head. "He will return soon and would like to meet you at the house."

With Maria Jesus' encouragement Joana and I decide to take a walk. We pass through the small village of five white houses nestled in the valley below the family's stretch of property. Each house is boarded on two or three sides by well tended plots of vegetables. Each house has out back its tall standing coop of chickens and other birds, their clucking and cooing gracing the quiet afternoon air. At one house an elderly woman bent over a cane comes out onto the front stoop. She leans against her cane and peers at us, her aged face the texture of dried figs. "Boa tarde, meninas," she says in a scratchy voice.

"Boa tarde, Senhora. How are your children? Have you heard from them lately?" Joana asks.

"Oh yes, they write regularly and the grocery woman in the next village reads the letters to me. Would you like to see a picture?"

She turns into the house and eventually comes back with a handful of black and white snapshots, worn and torn around the edges. Balancing precariously at the edge of the stoop she tells us detailed stories of her sons and daughters who now live in France, Belgium, Moçambique and Lisbon. Joana laughs with the funny parts, and I feel goose bumps along my arms at the sad stories. The old woman cries when she tells us about her granddaughter who died in a foreign land, even before she had a chance to see her.

"They buried her over there," she says. "I never held that baby."

Joana reaches out to embrace her and with great emphasis places a kiss on each cheek. Eventually we leave the old woman with her photographs and continue along the skinny hard-packed dirt road furrowed deep with wagon tracks. Out past the cluster of houses, family vineyards stretch in small rectangular plots over the low hills.

Joana says the village may soon disappear. All the inhabitants are old people, their bodies bent toward the earth they've tended for fifty or sixty years, their distinguished faces entirely weathered with wrinkles. The younger people have emigrated to Africa, France, or Switzerland or, like Joana's parents many years before, have moved off to the city. After the '74 coup freed Moçambique and Angola, many of them once again moved, some to Lisbon, others to Brazil. Joana says this land in the interior can no longer sustain entire families. Now it's only the old people who continue to cling to the only life they have ever known.

When we return to the house the caretaker, a

35

broad-shouldered short man of few words, goes off with Joana to talk about the grape harvest. I stand in the yard with the chickens until Maria Jesus steps out the back door and asks if I would like to see how she makes cheese. I follow her to a tiny back shed where she shows me a row of hand-size metal tins covered with cheesecloth.

"It's made from the goat's milk," she says. Picking up one of the tins, her bony elbows poking through her threadbare gray sweater, she flips the tin back and forth in her palms, excess cloudy white water dripping between her fingers. After a few minutes she places the tin again on the wooden board, the cheese inside now firmer and more set.

"May I try?" I ask.

"Oh, but the American girl will mess her nice hands."

"I would like to try." I pull my hair back behind my head and fasten it with a rubber band.

Maria Jesus hands me one of the containers and then takes one herself. "It's like this," she says.

I feel how runny the cheese is and wonder how she can do it without it all dumping onto the floor. As I flip it into my other hand I feel half the cheese slide out into my palm, and I make a face in her direction.

"It goes back and forth like this," she says. "Not too slow. Not too fast."

She starts on another one while I still struggle with the first, my hands moving slowly, tentatively. At the rate I'm going we'll have cottage cheese for supper. Finally Maria Jesus touches my shoulder lightly and intercedes, trying to show my awkward fingers the precise, simple movements of her skillful hands.

After dinner, while Joana and I take a quick coffee by the kitchen fire, Maria Jesus cleans up the dishes. I thank her again for teaching me about cheese. She says, "When the American girl comes again maybe she will teach me to read."

I think about how Maria Jesus and her husband have been married and in this same house for fifty some years. They've watched this same view out the window, greeted the same neighbors, followed the same routine of tending these vineyards and animals for nearly twice my lifetime. And I, since leaving my family's home fifteen years ago, have never lived in even one house longer than a year! There's something in me that yearns for stability. But as Joana has already explained, the life of this village is probably disappearing. Maybe already it only serves a nostalgic memory for Portuguese emigrants and myself.

* * * * *

The curves and turns in the darkened road jolt me back and forth as Joana speeds through the night, her body leaning smoothly into each curve, her relation to the road as familiar and steady as the long-lasting ties to her family and friends.

For miles we travel silently through the night until Joana speaks, her words placed like the brush of a Japanese painter, quick, sparse, exact. "I imagine you've gone through many changes in four years."

"Yes," I say, closing the silence around me again.

She says, "Let me tell you a story you've heard

before about Alexandra. You know her parents and mine have lived across the street from each other since they moved from that village, how our families have known each other for generations. It was Alexandra's father who helped deliver me when I suddenly decided to come into the world in the middle of the night. A few months later Alexandra was born, and even before we shared a spoken language already our communication was fast and deep. Leslie, that's how you and I have known each other, our friendship beginning way before you knew to speak my language."

Tears caress my cheek silently in the dark. Joana's hand seeks out mine and holds it warm for a moment.

I want to tell her everything, but I don't yet know the words of my uncertainty.

3

The bright red door swings open into a room filled with Kitaro's sky blue music. The morning light caresses the studio. I stand still in the doorway as Helena and Joana exchange greetings and kisses on each cheek. Then they turn back towards me, smiling.

"So you like it?" Joana asks.

"It's beautiful," I say, understanding immediately why both of them love to paint here. It's the perfect dream, this large room of white walls, large windows and skylights, high up in a building on a ridge overlooking the city to one side and a stretch of valley to the other.

"Come on in," Helena beckons. She places her warm hand along the side of my face and kisses my other cheek. "I've made coffee and arranged some pastries," she adds. "Let's eat, and then we can work."

"Will I get to see some of your drawings?" I ask.

"Of course. I'll show you in a while." She follows the words with a smile, familiar and sure.

Joana takes a seat at the small round table spread with one of the brightly colored tablecloths woven in the region and sold at the markets. As Helena prepares the coffee, I stand at the large window that encompasses both the view of Coimbra and a valley off to the side. I run my hand along the windowsill, listen to Joana and Helena exchange tidbits of news, and watch a scatter of birds move across the sky, their flight in graceful harmony with Kitaro. I think about Helena in the room behind me and I say to myself, like a lesson, *Be careful with your heart.*

Joana and Helena come again to a very familiar topic, their interest in putting on an exhibit.

"How many years have you talked about this, Joana?" I hold the small cup of very dark coffee near my chin so the warmth and heady aroma caress my face.

"Too long," she says as she puts two heaping spoonfuls of sugar into her demitasse, a drop of coffee, and rapidly stirs them together before topping it off with another swirl of coffee.

"It seems to be the only topic among everyone I know," Helena adds. "Under fascism none of us

40

showed our work for fear of reprisal. At least none of us that we know."

"But it's been years," I say, "since the government changed."

"I guess we haven't yet learned to speak past those generations of silence." Helena picks up a pastry that looks like a miniature mince pie.

"Can't you try now?" I ask.

"Maybe." Helena adds, as she looks across the table at Joana, the slight lift of her shoulders indicating, why not?

"Let's talk about it later," Joana says. "Why don't you show her your drawings now?"

Helena pulls down onto the floor long sheets of paper, some drawings made with pencil, others with felt markers and watercolor. As she lays them out I notice the thin gold chain around her wrist and the tawny color of her hand that begins to show a light network of lines from thirty some years of living. She says, "I try not to talk too much about my drawings, as I hope they speak for themselves."

Some are an abstract of color, some are portraits, many are clearly scenes beginning in this room and opening out through these windows to the view outside. Joana studies each of the drawings as if seeing them for the first time. She points out certain things she particularly enjoys, the intensity of color her greatest interest. I like the portraits, their exactness showing emotion in the subtle lines of a mouth, the glance of an eye, the way hands lay together on a lap. They speak to me the language of the body, a Portuguese sound.

Joana asks, "Leslie, can we sketch you today?"

41

"I'll feel embarrassed."

"It'll be fun," Helena says.

"Okay," I say. "What do I do?"

"You can sit there if you like." Helena touches her hand to my hip and nods in the direction of a midnight-blue chair.

Joana sits down with a large pad of paper, felt markers, and watercolor. Helena paces around the room mumbling about the light, the angle she wants, and whether she should use charcoal or markers.

"What am I supposed to do with my body?" I ask, not quite sure where to put my arms or how to hold my face, feeling my whole life will be evident in my expression.

Helena stops pacing and looks at me perched stiffly in this canvas chair. "Just relax."

"Does my hair look okay?" I run my hand along the back of my neck.

"Here, let me see." With both hands Helena brushes the curls back off my shoulders and then straightens my collar. I flush with the pleasure of her fingers light against the sides of my neck.

"Just sit comfortably," Helena says. She leans over and flips a new tape into her deck and soon George Winston moves lightly across the room.

"How do you know Kitaro and Winston?" I ask.

"I have friends from all over," Helena says. "They introduce me to the world's great diversity. This may be a small country, but we do hear more than just fados."

Helena sits on a high-legged stool a few feet from me and studies the sketch pad on her lap. She's wearing baggy cotton pants of a marvelous magenta and a pink Indian style cotton blouse tied with a deep purple sash, accentuating the reddish hue of her hair.

"Joana," I ask, "does your friend Helena always dress in such wild colors?"

Helena looks down at herself and then across at me, her eyes reaching mine with a swift ease. She smiles a wide-open grin.

"Helena wears on her body the colors I'm just getting the courage to paint!" Joana says.

The room quiets except for the graceful sound of Winston moving Winter into Spring. Joana and Helena bend over their work, glancing up at me between the motions of their hands. I sit very still, feeling quite self-conscious.

* * * * *

Joana calls in an excuse to work and we travel to the beach where I read a book and she spends a couple of hours painting. The warm sun, the constant rush of the waves, and Joana working at her easel in comfortable silence are the surest reasons I've come to Portugal.

After lunch at a small shop in the village square Joana and I return to the empty beach to walk along the shoreline as the tide turns inward towards land.

"Tell me one thing," Joana says as we start off along the sand, "has your heart recently been broken?"

"It's not characteristic of you to be so direct." I reach down to grab a handful of grainy sand that I let slowly slip through my fingers.

"I know. It's what I've learned from you," she answers.

43

Joana stops us in our tracks with the light touch of her hand. The wind off the ocean lifts her short black hair and scatters it about her head. She looks at me squarely.

I turn from her, reach into my pocket for one of the stones I picked up earlier, and toss it in a high arch towards the restless sea. "It's hard to talk about."

"I know."

"But there's so much you don't know."

"Then tell me."

I start to cry. We walk along the beach, the rough crash of waves a comfort of sorts.

"Does Miguel know I'm a lesbian?" I ask finally.

"We've never spoken directly about it, but I think he knows."

I lean up against a mass of gray black rock, my eyes filling again with tears. I think about the empty fog-draped streets of Provincetown where the lonesome cry of the foghorn measures the night, and about Deirdre in Boston with a new lover. I let the wind tangle my hair around my face for a moment before reaching up and pulling it back. Joana looks out over the water, her patience sure like the endless horizon. I could tell her nothing and still she would know something.

"It's hard to translate my experience into your culture," I say. "I don't know if you can understand."

"I can listen," she says, taking my arm in a firm grip and giving me a gentle shake.

"There's so much I've wanted to tell you about my most recent lover — it was so hard not being able to write you about it. There are entire sections of my life you don't know anything about. Like Deirdre. We were together for two years. But you didn't know that." I kick up a spray of sand. "We broke up four months ago and she won't even talk to me. She just ignores me!"

Joana wraps her arm around my neck and pulls me close to her for a brief moment. "I'm sorry." She reaches into the huge pocketbook slung across her shoulder and pulls out a handkerchief.

I unfold it and look at the letters J and M in a fancy embroidered script of tiny flowers. "I hate blowing my nose in something so beautiful." I wipe my eyes and cheeks, and then blow my nose.

"Does this relate to your break from political work too?" Joana asks.

"How do you always know the right questions?" I think about the winter night winds howling in Provincetown, the bare aloneness that awakened my terror and sent me running to Joana's side where time and distance have never hindered our clear understanding.

"Tell me what happened."

I take a deep breath and lean back against the cold rock. It's so hard to explain. I listen to the repeated crash of waves and the far cry of a gull overhead, my eyes closed to the light. When I look out again Joana is still standing in the same place, looking out towards the horizon.

"Deirdre and I met in New York. She wasn't into political work and I guess I was getting tired of it too. It's so easy to feel hopeless. So when she suggested we move to Cape Cod I decided it was a perfect way to take a break and get some sense of direction. But after a year I felt more disconnected than before. And when Deirdre left I realized I had no connections or focus. I don't know how to be in that country anymore."

"You were counting on somebody else," Joana says.

"It's not just that. There's something you can trust here, something wider than just the individual people around you." I mark off the landscape with a wide sweep of my hand. How hard it is to figure this out in English, much less to attempt a translation into Portuguese. "I don't feel any sense of continuity in the States." I step away from the cold gray rock and head along the edge of the water.

"I know it must be hard," Joana says, matching my stride.

"Take Deirdre. When things changed between us she didn't care to maintain our friendship. People there are like plastic, you throw them in the trash when you're through. You box them up and ship them off like that part of your life never existed. I can't stand it. Whenever I'm there, I feel like a foreigner, but I don't know if I can live here either."

"You can always live here," Joana says.

"Joana, I don't know if I can."

"What do you mean?"

"I'm a lesbian now."

"You're the same person I've always known."

"But my life is different."

"I don't understand," she says. "I try to, but I don't know if I understand." She puts a hand on one hip and looks off to the side quizzically.

"Imagine," I say, "if you were the only heterosexual and everybody you knew was gay. How would you feel about that?"

46

"I wouldn't mind," she says.

"But really imagine it," I say. "Everything in the world is gay, the television, motion pictures, all the books you read, everybody in your family and all of your friends, and you're the one person who's different. You wouldn't know Miguel and if you did you couldn't risk letting him know how you feel."

"Is it that strange for you?" Joana asks, a high flush coloring her cheeks.

"Not for me," I say. "I mean, I know who I am."

"You have so many friends here," she says. "I always want you to stay."

"Joana, what if I said I want to be lovers with you?" I pull together the sides of my silver jacket and zip it up fast, protecting myself from her answer.

"Well, you and I aren't like that, are we?" Her voice strains high against the afternoon air.

"Look at the point I'm making. If I live here will that mean giving up being with anyone? How will I ever meet other lesbians when everything is so hidden in this country?"

Joana shuffles her feet. She shoves her hands into her pockets and hunches her shoulders, bending her head slightly towards her chest. I don't know if she's mad or just thinking. We walk along quietly. A part of me wants to run away from all of this. I wish we hadn't taken this stupid ride to the beach. I wish we were sitting back at the house with all the kids around and Constança serving tea.

"I do know somebody," Joana says tentatively, "who maybe knows some women. I have this male friend who I think is homosexual. I mean, I'm not sure. And I don't know how I could ask."

"Maybe you could just introduce us."

"But what if I'm wrong?"

"I have experience in this, Joana. I can handle it," I say, impatient with her uncharacteristic caution.

"Well, I have experience with Portuguese men," she counters, "and I don't know if he can handle it."

I shoot back, "Maybe it's you that's having the problem."

"That's not fair." Joana stops walking. Standing firmly in place with her hands on her hips, she gives me a tenacious look. "You're giving me something to deal with that I've never had to deal with before and you expect me to be right on target, to know exactly what I'm doing. Well, I don't know."

"That's the whole point," I say. "If I stay here maybe there's no way for me to live as a lesbian, to be known and accepted for who I am!" Tears fill my eyes and dampen my cheeks in the chilly breeze. I start to turn away.

"Come here," Joana says, opening her arms. I bury my face in her bulky white sweater and smell the light touch of jasmine perfume. "Olha querida," she says several times, holding me tight like one of her children. "We'll figure it out," she says. "We'll figure it out."

* * * * *

Miguel is hunched over the table, dipping a pen into a small bottle of ink and moving it swiftly onto a sheet of paper where he is sketching something I can't see. The Miles Davis tape I gave him some years ago is playing quietly on a tape recorder on a shelf near his head. It pleases me to watch him swaying slightly with the rhythm of the music. Our

48

tastes are often quite different on many subjects, and I haven't always been successful at choosing something he enjoys.

He motions me into the room. "Come and have a seat and watch me struggle over a drawing." He instinctively runs his fingers back along the side of his temple, mapping out the line to where his jet black hair has receded.

Happily I pull up a chair, always glad to sit with him while he works. "I should have brought you a Walkman," I say, pointing to the tape recorder.

"I could use one some days on my rounds when I hear complaints about conditions at the hospital. What can you do in an economy faltering like this one?" Miguel rubs his fingers over the buttons where his white cotton shirt pulls a bit too taut. "Look at this." He picks up the drawing and holds it towards me. "For twenty years I've been trying to sketch this woman, but being a free spirit she always slips away."

I look at Joana holding a sketch pad and pen up against her chest. In her other hand she carries a baby doll and a plastic boa constrictor, both dangling next to her legs. I look at the direct gaze of Joana's eyes, her short dark hair brushed back away from her face, her mouth set firm. "That looks just like her," I say.

"I know. But something still is missing."

"Maybe she looks too serene," I suggest.

"That's how I always picture her." Miguel tosses the drawing onto his desk.

"But what about the contradiction?" I say.

"What contradiction?"

"The one you've drawn into the picture. Joana's

protectively holding art against her chest while a baby dangles from her other hand with a boa constrictor ready to strike."

"No. They're only toys," he says.

"But why did you draw them?"

"It's an image from a memory." Miguel shrugs, leans back in his chair, and props his feet on the edge of the desk. His face is pale and he looks tired, probably from too much work.

"There's something I want to talk to you about, Miguel." I grab a pencil and tap it along the edge of the table. How do I tell him? "Miguel, you might already know this . . . I want you to know because if I'm going to live here it's something I'm going to have to deal with. I'm a . . . I . . . I love women. I'm a homosexual. I'm a lesbian. God, I don't know how to tell you this in Portuguese!"

I look at his face, trying to read some expression, but don't see anything. "Miguel, did you know?"

"It always seemed women meant the most to you," he says in a measured tone.

"Your friendship is important to me too," I say.

"But men play a minor role in your life." Miguel picks up from the desk his rarely smoked pipe and a small folded bag of tobacco. He uncurls the bag and taps the pipe full of the flaky green brown leaves.

How can I explain my choices are as intrinsic to me as his choices are to him? At the same time, I'm resistant about having to explain. Yet as Joana said, how can I expect them to be on target with their response when they've never had to deal with this before?

I watch Miguel open a tiny matchbox, reach in with his large fingers and pick up a skinny wooden match. He strikes it and presses the flare against the bowl of his pipe, pulling the flame in with short, quick puffs. Finally I ask, "Miguel, how do you feel about it?"

"Me? I don't have any problem. I don't think I have any problem with it." He shifts in his chair, the sharp, sweet smell of tobacco filling the room as he sucks and puffs at the pipe. "You know," he continues, "Joana says she'd be bored being only with women. I think a person needs the diversity men and women offer each other. Maybe you haven't met the right man." He holds out his pipe and smiles towards me, the fading red ember of the tobacco counterbalancing the building flare of my impatience.

"Not everyone has that perspective," I say. "Sometimes I think women and men are different species and I'm amazed they can actually live together and get along."

"It's what's most natural —"

"Miguel," I say sharply. "Since when have you so narrowly defined —"

"I'm not saying what you do is unnatural." His voice is soft and conciliatory. "The male and female bodies are designed to go together for the propagation of the race. That's all I mean."

"Our options aren't limited to that," I say.

"I suppose not." Miguel swings his feet from the table top to the floor and reaches down to straighten the legs of his pants. Sitting back in his chair, he folds his arms across his chest and gives me a sideward glance. "Leslie, you don't expect to meet anyone, do you? I mean, there probably aren't any homosexuals here."

"You mean in all of Portugal?" I say.

51

"I mean in Coimbra, maybe there aren't any in Coimbra."

"Then I'll go to Lisbon."

"How would you know where to look?"

"I don't know. I've never done this in another country. In the U.S. you just kind of know. There are women's bookstores and social events. Sometimes I strike up a conversation with someone I think is gay."

"How do you know?" he asks.

"In the U.S. I often can tell by looking, but I don't know what it's like here. Everything is so invisible."

"You know, sometimes people don't want to know these things," Miguel says.

"Do you mean you wish I hadn't told you?"

"I mean you could get in trouble talking like this with people you don't know well."

"But I'm talking with you," I say, "not anyone else."

"Joana knows, doesn't she?"

"I told her during my last visit. Miguel, are you upset I told you?"

"No," Miguel says. "You know I'm an open person, Leslie."

"I thought you might have a stronger reaction," I say. I don't tell him but there's something about this that feels too easy.

4

Eleven years ago, after the military coup, big political debates would ensue over dinner at Alexandra and Tiago's. Joana once told me her two friends were Communist Party card holders way before the coup ended fascism. She said this was probably their attempt to be part of the liberal avant-garde. But I knew her laugh was a way of trying to cover over a memory that never went away.

In their third year at the university Alexandra and Joana were sitting in the cafeteria going over notes for an art history exam when a school administrator summoned Alexandra into the hallway. Joana said she remembered seeing the door slowly close behind them and a quick glimpse of an ordinary-looking man in a brown suit with a thin black strip of cloth around one of his arms, signifying a death in the family. Joana couldn't see him well, but wondered if he was one of Alexandra's uncles from the interior. She thought to go and ask if anything was wrong with the grandparents who were very old. But when she walked to the door a few minutes later they were already gone.

When it was time for class and Alexandra hadn't returned, Joana gathered up their books and headed off for the exam. Joana told the professor about the brown-suited man and that maybe a family emergency had come up for her friend. The professor's short nod of dismissal haunted Joana for years afterwards, making her wonder if he had been an accomplice.

No one saw Alexandra for five weeks, though eventually her parents were told she was being held for questioning. The father immediately had a heart attack and though he survived he was never the same. Tiago nearly went insane, pacing continually outside police headquarters. Joana eventually withdrew from school that year because she was terrified of the blank stares of passing strangers.

When Alexandra was finally released she went immediately to the family home in the interior. There she ate potatoes, fish, and greens until she added pounds to a figure that had always been slight. She retired to bed early and rose late, sat by the fire with her grandparents, and tried to move through her nightmares. No one outside the family ever heard the stories, not even Joana, with whom Alexandra usually shared everything.

The next year they returned quietly to the university, with less laughter and with caution in their eyes. Supposedly the two card holders gave up their political association. But a rebellion raged behind their silence, to be shouted in hot debates across the dining room table after the 1974 coup. Still, only with the most intimate of friends.

This evening's dinner party is in my honor. Since my arrival Alexandra, Tiago, and their daughter, Rosalina, have been on holiday in Brussels. The moment they returned Alexandra telephoned and made arrangements for this evening. It's a quick ride of a couple of blocks to their new home. Miguel parks the car just outside the walkway's tall, ornate metal gate, and the kids and I pile out of the back seat. The two-story house is surrounded by a thick wall that reaches above my head. It looks as though it's been recently cleaned of scrawled slogans and political posters. Miguel pulls the gate back on screeching hinges and holds it as we enter into the landscaped garden. To the right an oblong arched wooden trellis bears trimmed grapevines. On the left bushes form a horseshoe around a curved stone bench and shallow cement pond. Between this and the house several fan-shaped trellises hold rose bushes. The outside of the house is an unadorned light pink stucco with tall, rectangular windows. A single line of azulejos, blue painted tiles characteristic of early Arabic influence, decorate the doorway.

Alexandra greets us at the door in a floor length light blue silk kimono that moves silently with her graceful motions. Her black hair is long and straight and tied to the side with a dangling piece of dark blue ribbon.

"Leslie, it's so nice to see you." She holds out her arms and wraps me in an embrace of smooth silk, the side of her face pressed lightly against mine.

"Alexandra, this is beautiful," Isabel says, taking the silk between her fingers. "Where did you get it?"

"Tiago brought it from one of his business trips."

"Oh, Alexandra, do you think he would arrange something for me sometime?" Isabel asks.

"Now, Isabel," Miguel interjects.

"Hello, hello, hello." Tiago walks into the foyer. "Bem-vindo, Leslie! Good evening everyone!" He takes my hand between his large hands and holds it firm for a moment. "Alexandra has made a great dinner for this evening." Tiago's tall, big-boned body stands erect, his shoulders held back at a sharp angle.

We take off our jackets and put them on the pegs of the large wooden frame that hangs against the wall. It's an intricately carved replica of the decorative yokes used to harness oxen in the field. Along the opposite wall hang lace handiwork mounted in glass frames, several gold filigreed hearts of various sizes suspended from gold chains, and an assortment of hand painted azulejos, each with a different design. Below this display is a high gloss wooden table with a marble top on which sit terra cotta pottery, a large platter, a bowl, and several vases.

"Alexandra has become quite a collector of the local artisans," Tiago tells me as we all walk down the hallway.

In the living room Paulo rises from the couch and

comes to shake our hands. "Boa noite," he says, the tips of his handlebar mustache bouncing lightly.

Teresa smiles and waves at us from the couch where she sits holding a glass of wine. A large tapestry hangs on the wall behind her head, depicting an ancient courtly scene.

"Where are the children?" Joana asks.

"We left ours with Teresa's mother," Paulo says.

"Rosalina is in her bedroom. Why don't you girls go find her?" Alexandra says to Isabel and Cristina.

During dinner the kids sit in front of the television with plates in their laps, watching the end of a comic Brazilian variety show. We sit in the dining room eating a thick soup of potatoes, carrots, cabbage, pork, and fish. This is followed by a heaping platter of steaming rice, croquettes of codfish, a salad of sliced tomatoes and black olives, and the thick, heavy bread called broa.

"Alexandra wants to make sure you don't forget the life of the common people," Paulo says, biting into a hunk of broa.

"The food is delicious," I say. "Thank you, Alexandra."

We talk about the weather, the food, Teresa's pregnancy, the recent Belgium trip, and my plans for employment. As we near the end of our second helping Tiago leans back in his chair and looks at me across the table. We smile at each other.

"So, Leslie," he says. "What do you think of this U.S. hostage situation in Lebanon?"

"I think the U.S. government is rather arrogant in its response."

"Good," he says. "I see your politics are still reputable."

57

"Why would they be anything different?" Alexandra asks Tiago, smiling first towards me and then towards Joana.

"With four years in the States," Tiago says, "who's to say what influences might do to anyone."

"I'm frightened of the situation in the Middle East," Teresa says, leading the conversation back to a serious thread.

Before we launch off into a complex and opinionated discourse, Rosalina calls from the other room, "The show is starting."

We leave the dishes on the table and sit in the lush chairs in the living room for the latest episode of "Blue Thunder," and American series about a helicopter and its macho crew. All conversation ceases for the duration. I pass the time trying to tune out the TV's loud blaring English, and thinking about Tiago's comment on my politics. I have made changes. How else could I respond to life in the eighties? But would Tiago understand?

When the set is finally turned off Tiago opens a bottle of port and Alexandra brings in a platter filled with figs and roasted chestnuts, shortbread cookies and marmalada. I keep waiting for the conversation to heat up, wondering what latest political controversy will be discussed. Instead, the three teenage girls push me for details on characters from the show "Dallas," while the adults carry on a hot debate about their choices for favorite sit-com of the past several months. I tell Zé and the girls I don't watch these programs back home. They don't believe me. The wide selection of shows is a recent and exciting experience for them, a window out of the boundaries of their small country. I want to warn them against this massive influence. But I already know what Joana will say: Sometimes you need a break from relentless reality.

*****

I am standing in a little garden that runs alongside a street stretching the length of two or three city blocks. Along the edge of this narrow garden is a waist-high concrete wall that protects walkers from the long rocky drop off. Out beyond the wall small mountains unfold east into a dusky blue. The houses of a distant village gather around a church steeple that stands like a sentinel.

The walkway that traverses the length of this park is made of small black and white stones inlaid in a variety of patterns. When I follow this path past a stone fountain, I come to the end of the garden and enter the Rua do Penedo da Saudade. It's a skinny street that winds down below the concrete wall, an entranceway into a valley that runs off to greet the distant hills. I remember a story about a prince who had a forbidden lover named Inês. After secret liaisons they would bid farewell to each other at this very spot that is now called the rock of yearning. In an effort to terminate his intense passion, the prince's family finally had the woman killed. He had her buried in Coimbra, at a place you can still visit, though I've never been there. Many people say his passion never died.

It was in this country of yearning, where emotions are a multi-textured, deep-hued fabric, that I myself came to open my heart and live life with a new intensity. I love this country. I don't want to go back to America, but I don't know if I can live here as a lesbian.

After last night, feeling American culture projected from the television screen into the midst of my friends, I am frightened that maybe passion can die, numbed out by this insidious effect of mass produced images. Maybe there is no place to live anymore. Maybe passion's only a nostalgic memory.

* * * * *

Several days after having dinner at Alexandra and Tiago's spacious house we arrive at Paulo and Teresa's small apartment where the group has reconvened. We're wall-to-wall people as the kids sprawl everywhere on the living room floor and the women fill the couch and few chairs. The men gather around a small sideboard as Tiago opens a bottle of port he brought with him. We're waiting for Helena to arrive.

I'm amazed how easily I keep up with the conversation, even with two or three people always talking at once. Suddenly I'm neither faltering over the Portuguese nor straining to understand. The words speed out of my mouth before I have a chance to wonder how I can understand enough to speak like this.

Teresa, Joana, and I are crowded together on the small couch. Two of Teresa's little ones take turns climbing into my lap to tell me stories, putting their little faces right next to mine. I love this closeness where proximity is measured in heartbeats instead of miles.

Helena arrives with cheeks a blush of red from

the night wind. She's wearing a knee-length dark gray coat that dips and sways with her body as she reaches to hug and kiss the people nearest her. She waves and gives a big smile to the gathering of women before Paulo pulls her into the circle of men.

Tiago pours port into tiny glasses on the sideboard and I watch them toast the evening. After the click of glasses Helena looks over he shoulder straight at me. I grin back and then catch Miguel watching us, his serious face not matching the jovial mood of the other men.

"Are we ready to go?" Joana asks the group. "I don't want to be late."

"I'm more than ready," Miguel says.

Teresa and Paulo's four small children stay at the house with Constança, whom we brought to baby-sit. We're going to an exhibit featuring an old university professor and a new young man who has just returned from Barcelona. Before I can get to Helena's side Paulo pulls her away from the group and Isabel grabs my hand to ask me to ride with her and Rosalina in Tiago's car. I catch a glimpse of Helena's face in the window as Paulo speeds by. Our cars play chase through the night streets.

Our group fills the nearly empty gallery with a boisterous appreciation. I see the older man's work is more traditional, but of a very fine quality. The younger man is quite avant-garde for this audience. His wide, bold, larger-than-life nude figures are abstracts of white and black skin against backgrounds of deep lavender, fluorescent green, or burnt orange.

Helena says, "We definitely need to do an exhibit. I want to show you can be avant-garde without leaving the country." She's wearing crystal blue

61

harem pants, a big sleeve aquamarine blouse with a low cut neckline, and blue ballet slippers. Her hair rides thick and untamed about her head. From one ear dangles a gold ring, the other carries a brightly colored plaster parakeet.

Joana takes a step back, looks Helena over closely, and says, "But you always leave for your short excursions, and each time you come back looking more yourself like a piece of art."

"Yes, that's true," Helena says, throwing her head back in a laugh.

"I want to help with the show," I say.

"Of course," Helena says. "The three of us will meet Wednesday to talk about it. Okay?"

After the exhibit twelve of us meet around three tables pushed together at the Café Muro. I love watching the teenagers and adults share an evening so naturally, everyone giving opinions equally. We all discuss the young painter, some of us a bit envious of his bold work, others challenged. We make such a scene that everyone in the place is enjoying our company. The talking never stops! This is what I love!

Helena is across the table and a few seats down from me, between Paulo, who keeps telling slightly lewd jokes, and Alexandra, who sits regally silent and unruffled. I enjoy watching the easy playfulness Helena shares with our friends. While everyone around the table is excitedly discussing the possibility of organizing an exhibit, Helena and Paulo end up virtually nose to nose in a heated debate about women's rights.

Helena says, "Maybe we should just do a women's show."

Everyone starts talking at once. I already have a big grin on my face when Helena looks in my direction and winks, and an uncontrollable joy fills me.

* * * * *

Lying in bed, the evening like a dance in my memory, I keep saying to myself, Be careful with your heart. But my heart seems not to listen.

I feel warm and comfortable, images of the evening filling me like a drink whose rush heats my insides. I move my hand onto my belly and feel my palm against the warm smoothness of my stomach. I run my hand up across my breasts, a fresh tingle following my fingertips. My other hand slides into the warmth between my thighs. I play along the edge of my underpants and then up across the cloth as my hips rise to greet my fingers. I slide under the elastic band and enter the wetness of my slick skin, caressing slow and sure.

I drift with the motions, pleasure charting its course like gulls soaring between land and sea. I could move all night with these currents. Until, suddenly, I surprise myself with an image of touching Helena's aquamarine blouse and kissing her lips. Oh, God, I can't think about this.

I pull my hand out from under the covers and recite again my promise to steer away from attractions for a while. I need a break and anyway she's Portuguese! There's no way anything can happen so don't even think about it.

Still . . . I return my hand to the warm covers, caressing and encouraging the fullness deep inside my body, my hips rocking and rising into the air, images of those I love careening through my head, and the possibility, the possibility of something, building into a full strong climax where, suddenly, Helena flashes through my brain.

As I drift into sleep I remember Paulo talking about the young painter. "He must be a faggot," he said.

5

The next morning I find on the table in the foyer
a letter from the U.S. Though there's no return
address I recognize Sarah's handwriting. I pick up the
envelope and stuff it into my pocket. Joana and
Miguel won't be back until lunch, so I decide to take
a walk. I don't want to open the letter yet. I already
imagine what it will say. Sarah will be wondering if
I've thought any further about her invitation to
return to the Catskills and to take a room in her
collective household. Decisions will have to be made,
she'll say. She'll wonder if my friends are still the

same as before. I'm wondering if she'll give me news about Deirdre, and I don't want to know. I don't want to think about America, I say to myself in repeated rhythm as I walk across the cobblestones.

I wander aimlessly through the streets until I stumble across the Jardim Botânico. As I descend the wide stone stairs into the central garden the cooler air and fresh earthy smell calm me a bit. The well-tended green plants with their identifying plaques and the flowers laid out in a series of geometrical patterns give a nice visual order, in contrast to my chaotic feelings.

Did I think I could let my past slip out of my life, the very thing for which I criticize my American friends? I am an American, but my friends there are totally so. I'm not anymore. I speak a language that often doesn't translate. I don't want to feel like this, always losing a part of myself to either side of the ocean.

I sit in the central garden, watching the men in their gray button down overalls tending to the plants and the garden paths. I walk back to the deeper part of the garden, its descending walkway into the dense ferns and tall trees a companion in my memories and dreams. But there, across the entranceway to my fond memory, is an ornate metal gate with a sign that says NO ENTRANCE. I know of a second way in and so continue along the curving path, only to encounter a simple metal link chain with a similar sign.

I follow the walkway back to the flower beds laid out in a star pattern around the central fountain. The red, yellow and pink flowers whose names I don't know are a pleasant contrast to the gray skies and cold chill that I imagine has begun to touch New

66

England. Today is Halloween in the United States. I've nearly reached the halfway mark of my round trip ticket. Soon I'll have to make a real decision. Will I cash the ticket in or return to the States? Sarah's unopened letter waits in my pocket, and I'm afraid of its influence and my indecision. I exit the garden, sad for the closure of its most beautiful walkway. I follow the streets back to Joana's with a familiar feeling of going home, yet accompanied by a shadow of doubt. Am I running away as Sarah says and closing off my own essential path?

* * * * *

Joana and I stretch out in the living room, she on the couch in the skirt and sweater she wore to school this morning, me on the floor in blue jeans and a flannel shirt. Everyone else has gone off to work or school. Constança is in the kitchen cleaning up the dishes from lunch.

Joana says, "I saw you received a letter from America."

"I haven't read it," I say.

"You haven't told them yet that you're staying, have you?"

"No," I say, wondering if I should tell Joana I'm still not certain what I want to do.

"Want to see if I can translate the letter?"

I pull the folded envelope out of my pocket and hand it up to her.

"Let's see." She glances over the first page with a look of perplexity. "This is funny. I don't understand anything of the first few sentences."

"Read them to me," I say.

"Dear Leslie, you missed a bad time last night. Marian and Suky dropped by. We smoked a doobie of some really fine shit and went cruising chicks for a super fine evening."

I start to laugh.

"What are they talking about?" Joana asks.

"She's just playing around," I explain. "What she says is they smoked some marijuana and went out somewhere, probably dancing."

"Cruising chicks means dancing?" Joana asks.

I give a hearty laugh and roll over onto my stomach. "This translation is too hard."

"Want me to read more?"

"Okay."

"We do miss you. Why haven't you written? Are you moving in over there or what? We'd really like you to live with us, but we don't know how long we can hold the room open."

Joana pulls away from the letter. "These are the people you were talking about, aren't they?"

"Yes."

"Do you miss them?"

"I don't know. I'd like to live with them, but I have my doubts about living in the States. You know, Joana, I communicate more clearly with you in an adopted language than I do with the people in my own country."

Joana looks over the top of the letter at me sprawled on the floor. "What if you'd never come here?"

"I'd be an entirely different person."

"Maybe just like them," she says.

I sit up and bend forward to touch my toes,

68

stretching the muscles in my back. "It's hard to think my life would be anything different," I say. "I guess I'm not sorry about feeling out of place. It's strange how living outside of my own country made me a foreigner to it. Who knows, maybe I'd be a foreigner there even if I'd never lived here."

"It gave you a wider perspective."

"That's true."

"What do you think it'd be like for me if I lived in the United States?"

"I can't imagine."

"I think I would like it," Joana says. "There's so much diversity there."

"It feels all the same to me," I say. "Joana, don't you want to go for a walk?"

"No, and don't change the subject." She leans off the couch and jiggles my foot. "You need to think about this Portuguese-American split you carry around. There are good things for both sides, you know? Like how you're able to make choices there that you can't make here."

"What choices?"

"Like education or jobs. From what you say a person can change careers, explore entirely different fields of interest. Here Zé is already having to decide what he's going to do for the rest of his life. This country's so small and that creates a lot of pressure. You and I have made different choices in our lives and that enriches our friendship. What you offer me is the freedom of your life and I offer you the stability of mine. What each of us yearns for is realized in many ways through this friendship. Maybe it's that balance you need to find between the country of your birth and this country of your heart. You can't turn away completely from there because a part of you will always need that connection."

"Yes, I like being out of the closet in the U.S., which I can't be here."

"Out of what closet?"

"Oh, Joana," I say. "Sometimes words are not enough to leap between our two cultures!"

When Joana goes to answer the phone I fold the pages of the letter, most of it still unread, and slide it back into the envelope. I see the postscript written in red ink and pull the letter back out, unfold it, and read the back page.

Deirdre wrote last week asking for your address. I hope you don't mind that I gave it to her. She says she's trying to mend her ways. It was lousy how she just stopped talking to you. But, if she does write, don't think it's more than it is. I hear she's still real tight with her new lover. Oh well, maybe you're over her by now.

6

Through various contacts I've arranged several private English lessons. Miguel and Joana won't take money for rent, so my living expenses have been very low, but at least I can help pay for food. There's a possibility of doing an English discussion group through Cristina's school, which would then give me enough of an income to move out on my own. It's a little scary, but Miguel said I probably can share a place with some students from the university. That'll make it easier and cheaper.

Once I've moved it's for real I'm living here and

71

not just visiting. Though I've lived in Coimbra, that was years ago, and now the change seems more frightening than exotic.

* * * * *

Helena invites me to join her and António and Susana, friends I haven't yet met, for a Sunday afternoon excursion into the countryside. We pack into a straw basket thick pork sandwiches, tomatoes and salty green olives, big yellow apples, a bottle of wine, and a box of sweet cakes filled with cream.

"Helena and I have known each other since we were children," António says as he drives along the winding roads into the interior.

"Of course I'm older than he is," Helena says. "It was usually me who had to baby-sit when our mothers took us to the beach. António was infamous for jumping in over his head."

"You saved my life a hundred times from the old nanny my father insisted on bringing down from England."

"His father is British," Susana says.

"That explains the sandy color," I say, noting his hair parted on the side and trimmed to his ears and the edge of his collar. His bangs are brushed in a sideward arch to reveal a high forehead, a thin long face, and a constant wide grin that offsets his serious square jaw.

"Did you notice he's pierced one of his ears," Helena says.

António reaches over to the passenger side to poke Helena in the ribs.

"He isn't really as wild as he tries to look,"

Helena says in a mock whisper towards me in the back seat.

Susana leans her wide, big-boned face next to mine and says into my ear, "Don't believe her."

"How did you and António meet?" I ask Susana.

"We met at the university."

Just past the first village we stop the car for several minutes as a boy of about fourteen, dressed in long pants, a black poncho and beret, herds fifty or so sheep down onto the road from a rocky path. The sheep swarm over the road and head along the pavement towards a second path a hundred yards in front of us. We roll down the windows and listen to the baying of the animals. I watch the last of them scamper over the edge of the road as we drive by.

"That boy's life must be so different than ours," I say. "It seems people like ourselves have more in common." I look at my companions in the car and realize they could easily be mistaken for Americans.

"You probably have a smoother adjustment coming into this country than that boy would have entering our world at the university," Susana says. She takes a small mirror and tube out of her purse and, with a sure hand, replenishes her lips a bright crimson. From a compact she retrieves a small pad to heighten the blush along her cheeks. Absent-mindedly she touches a finger to the edge of her eyelid where blue shadow reaches out into a curved tip.

Once gain the car slows as we come upon a group of people making a slow procession along the main road. Many of them carry colorful bouquets of flowers.

"It's probably the local saint's birthday," Susana says.

We inch around the large gathering. Old men and women, children, and people of our own age march along, a surge of people dressed in black. From the smiles and the gaiety of the flowers it's a joyful celebration.

At the front of the procession four men dressed in formal suits carry a cloth-draped platform on which sits a white and blue statue about three feet high, garlanded in flowers. A priest, robed in white, walks in front holding aloft a golden cross.

As we pull past the crowd Helena asks, "Leslie, have you ever been to Fátima?"

"Years ago, when I lived here," I say.

"Maybe you'd like to make a trip there with me sometime."

"What penance do you have to make?" António asks.

"Nothing, of course. I want to do some sketching," Helena says.

"Do you suppose any of those people's prayers are ever answered?" António asks.

"What amazes me," I say, "is the determination of people who walk for days in pilgrimages to Our Lady of Fátima. I remember seeing groups camped at the side of the road, cooking and sleeping under plastic sheets. Always there was such perseverance and conviction in their eyes."

"It seems what they believe in is outside of themselves," Susana says.

"Maybe," I say, "but something carries them through."

At the edge of the third village we turn onto a dirt and stony road and bounce up a steep embankment to a deserted castle. As António skids to a halt in a pasture, I look out the window at the huge fortress of boulder and stone. It takes my breath away to think that once people actually lived here.

We leave the car and walk through an arched opening in the ten foot high wall surrounding the courtyard where two goats roam freely, eating the bright green grass. The castle is three stories high. I see through the window openings that its walls are two or three feet thick. Pushing open the massive wooden door we enter into a room as wide and long as half a football field. On either end huge fireplaces extend nearly the full width of the building.

"I always think how cold it must have been," António says.

We climb among the stone staircases and wide open rooms that are chilly from lack of sunlight. I climb narrow winding stairs and find myself alone on top of a watchtower. I lean against the parapet, where the stones have been warmed by the sun. The view stretches over the rolling countryside, a green patchwork of fields and clusters of trees. Centuries ago this watchtower must have served the perfect defense in sighting encroaching enemies. I feel the ancient thick stone under my hands and wonder why romance is so often represented by such huge fortresses. I watch the goats graze in the courtyard. Then I join Susana and António who have spread out a blanket in the sun. Helena joins us and we open up our picnic lunch.

"Helena tells us you lived here some years ago," António says. "Your Portuguese is quite good."

"Thank you. Though I'm afraid it gets rusty with lack of use."

"What did you do when you were here?" Susana asks.

"I taught English and worked with a group of people organizing peasants in the villages around Coimbra."

"With the Grupo de Animação?" Helena asks with excitement in her voice.

"Yes."

"I heard about that group. I was living in Porto at the time and not really involved like I am now, so my interest wasn't strong enough for me to catch a train and come down to meet them," Helena says. "Do you keep contact with the people?"

"No. That was another life ago."

"So what are your plans now?" António asks.

"I'm pretty certain I'm going to make Portugal my home again, so I want to find a place to live."

"I know of a place," António says. He tells us about a group of people who live in a huge old house, entertaining us for half an hour with the details of their quirks and eccentricities and the very involved history of their household.

Helena says, "Why don't I know about this house and these people?"

Susana says, "He probably is making the whole thing up."

"No. It really is true, and it's the perfect place for Leslie to live."

"Oh, António, you're making it up," Susana says. She leans over and tickles his stomach. He grabs her arm and pulls her close and they roll into the grass. Susana escapes and runs towards the castle entrance. António follows.

"Do your friends plan to marry?" I ask.

"I don't know. António likes to do things differently. What he was telling you about the house is probably his dream of living collectively with other people. He doesn't really believe in marriage."

I look towards the castle and see Susana and António framed in a window. They lean into each other for a long kiss, the sun glinting off António's small gold earring.

Helena turns to look. "António's such a hippy and Susana's family is so traditional," she says, "I don't know if they'll ever work it out."

"So tradition still has its strong influence."

"The boundaries of what's accepted are not as wide as in the U.S." Helena says. "António would like to live with Susana and he wishes he had the nerve to grow his hair long."

"Maybe he will someday," I say, wondering if I myself can live openly in a culture not my own. I watch Helena pick up the bottle of wine and place it to her lips. I should just tell her I'm a lesbian. She'll probably have no problem with it and if she does, well, it will take an edge off this attraction. I watch her wipe the corners of her mouth with a napkin and I try not to think about how nice it would be to kiss her. I should just tell her.

Before I have a chance António shouts out the window, "Hey you two, come and join us."

On the return trip I sit beside Helena in the back seat. António turns on the tape recorder and Simon and Garfunkel sing us back into town. Outside of Helena's house we sit in the car and talk for a few minutes. She asks me to come in and António gives an encouraging nod.

The apartment is predominately warm browns and

encompassing, quite different from the studio, which is airy and wide open in its space.

"I'm glad you came up," she says. "I wasn't quite ready to be alone. Come into the kitchen and I'll make some tea." Helena puts a kettle onto the stove.

"It was a pleasant day," I say.

"António and Susana are such dear friends," Helena explains, placing shortbread cookies on the table. "It's nice to have friends like that, don't you think?"

"Yes," I say, feeling awkward about where to stand or what to do with my hands.

Helena takes a cookie and offers the package towards me. "What did you do for employment in America?"

"I've lived all over the country and done all kinds of work — construction, restaurant, clerical. I've taught self-defense and worked in a hospital."

"I think it would be nice to have so many experiences."

"Including going crazy with too many choices! I've done a little bit of everything, but maybe not quite enough in any one thing."

"I see what you mean. I've taught art to children for twelve years and feel good about the concentration I've had. It's helped my own work. You don't do any kind of art?"

"No, but I appreciate it."

"Maybe we can talk sometime about the work you did here in Coimbra. It would be great if we could collaborate on something. I could use the help," Helena gets up to get the water.

"I'm not sure I have anything to offer," I say.

"Everyone does," she says as she pours the

steaming water into a teapot. "Let's go into the other room. It's more comfortable."

We sit on opposite ends of the couch and talk until Helena pulls out a photo album and sits next to me, opening the wide book across both of our laps. Her thigh touches lightly along my thigh. Her smooth voice, so near my ear, opens my desire. I remind myself that being this close doesn't necessarily mean anything. Even strangers sit this close on crowded trains and buses. Still, I want to wrap my arms around her.

Helena points out various photos from her travels and tells amusing stories that make us both laugh. I enjoy sitting next to her, but when the last page is turned I jump up with a sudden excuse about the time and the need to get back to Joana's.

"Let's get together soon," Helena suggests easily as we say goodbye.

Outside, in the early evening light, I walk a deserted street to the corner where I catch the streetcar. As the car rumbles across the cobblestones my mind races with thoughts. I want to rein in my feelings, stop opening to this attraction. How would I even explain to her how I'm feeling? I don't know the right Portuguese words, and I definitely don't know the Portuguese reality of loving women. As the streetcar screeches to a halt at the next stop I think, It's better not to get into a complication and set myself up for disappointment.

* * * * *

Several of us meet at Joana and Miguel's to begin discussing the organization of an exhibit.

Raul, a colleague of Joana's from school, says, "I want to see this happen."

"Let's talk first about practical things," Miguel says. "What kind of space we'll need, advertising, who to exhibit, things like that."

"No. I think we should start out with what kind of theme we want," Alexandra interjects, her long thin fingers emphasizing with a graceful motion.

"Why don't you do a show for kids?" Isabel yells down from upstairs.

"I think we should be really open," Joana says as she runs her hands back through her short black hair. "Let's make this show about freedom of expression. Anybody can exhibit and they can exhibit whatever they want."

"Don't you think we need some kind of control?" Raul asks, his eyebrows and forehead wrinkled in serious concentration.

"No," Joana states.

"But we have to determine space use," Miguel explains. He crosses one leg over the other, leans forward, and lays one arm across his knee.

"Okay. Okay." Joana says. "Why don't I disappear until you guys figure out the practicals and then you can call me back to talk about freedom." She gets up from her chair and shakes the wrinkles out of her skirt.

"Joana, don't leave," Helena says.

"I'll be back. I'm just going to get more coffee." She smiles at us and heads towards the kitchen.

Two hours later we have the basics mapped out; who's going to check out gallery space; who's going to design the advertising; how to select the entries; and a title for the exhibit.

"That wasn't so hard," I say to Helena as she finishes her coffee, enjoyment clear in her dark brown eyes.

"I'm excited about it," she says. "You know, you were the one who helped us take this seriously."

"You just needed a little push," I say.

"Then how about if I give you some encouragement in return? I'd love it if you'd come and see our work in the villages. I'm sure it would interest you."

"I don't know," I reply, threatened by the possibility. "I don't know if I'm still confident about that kind of work."

"Why don't you come to my apartment and we can talk," Helena says. "António and Susana are coming over and afterwards I can bring you home."

"It would be nice to talk."

"I'm sure you have a lot brewing inside," Helena says.

"Maybe too much," I say.

The two of us make our departure from the group and walk to Helena's car at the end of the block. Helena revs up the motor and turns out into the street. "So tell me your story," she says.

"I don't know why I'm being so resistant."

"You can trust me, Leslie. I'm not going to make you sign onto a comrade brigade or join some political party! I just feel we have some things in common."

"Since I returned to the States," I say, "It's been difficult to know how to belong or what to do. For years I worked with all kinds of groups. I've marched against bigotry and nuclear warheads. I've done community organizing with poor people and government lobbying to change laws, but during the past year or so I've dropped everything."

"It's hard to keep your spirit up, isn't it?" Helena murmurs.

"Everything in the States is so overwhelming — all my efforts seem so insignificant I don't know where best to put my energies.

"Whatever you do is important," Helena says.

"I used to say that myself, but I've lost perspective."

"What have your interests been the past couple of years?"

"I drift from one thing to the next with no particular focus or direction. It seems I don't have the words any more to describe my reality."

"So how can you break through silence, make a new language, a new perspective?" Helena slows the car as a couple of barefoot boys in ragged clothes scoot across the street in front of us.

"I don't know what you mean," I say, irritated at her insistence.

"What's the use of having an experience," she says, "if you don't try to interpret it into a form that can be shared with other people?"

"But it's a contradiction to break silence in order to speak of silence."

"Sometimes you Americans think too much with your heads and you forget about your hearts." Helena's voice is impatient.

"You don't live in America. You don't know what it's like!" I feel myself racing inside.

Helena touches her hand to my arm and adds in a subdued tone, "Leslie, maybe you need to trust that sometimes somebody else might know what's good for you."

I look out the window and take in a deep breath to calm myself. "Excuse me for being short-tempered. What you're saying is exactly what I need to be listening to."

* * * * *

António has on black pants and a bright yellow and orange tie-dyed T-shirt that he covered with a sweater on his way over. Susana sits at the table in skin tight blue jeans and a baggy blue sweater, rolling joints. Helena puts Kitaro into the tape deck.

Susana joins me on the rug. She lights up one of the joints and passes it to me. I inhale deeply as António and Helena join us. "I've never been stoned in Portugal," I say, amazed at this new experience.

"I like knowing an American," Susana says.

"Yes, and Helena likes Americans too," António adds as Helena jabs him in the side.

"She wants me to get involved in her village work," I say quickly, trying to ignore António's comment.

"Let's speak English," Susana says.

"I prefer Portuguese," I say.

Susana and António branch off into English while Helena and I continue on in Portuguese, all of us talking together. I feel the pot start to lighten my arms and chest. I begin to laugh at the mix of languages and soon can't tell which is which. The words come out of my mouth one by one in three dimensional letters.

Suddenly António's playing a flute and the music runs a silver river along my spine and through my chest. Helena's leaning back against the couch. Susana's sitting close to me, rocking back and forth, her long legs stretched out in front of her, her wide feet now bare. The pleasure in me is so strong that the two languages converge and with these new friends I feel the joining of my Portuguese and American self. This is too intense. I stand up and find my way to the kitchen where I drink a large glass of cold water and then refill the glass, holding its slight chill against my forehead. I lean against the sink and feel goodness pumping through my body in a warm rush.

"Are you all right?" Helena asks.

"Oh, yes." I set down the glass and turn towards her.

"You're crying."

"It's only because I feel so good. I feel so good," I say. "I wish I could tell you."

Helena wraps her arms around me in one full sweep, the full length of our bodies finally touching each other. I bring my arms up around her back and feel my pleasure multiply.

"I'm so happy too," she says close to my ear. She brings her hand up to the back of my neck and places her lips against my cheek for a light kiss.

I don't want to cry, but I can't stop. Helena holds me for a moment as the sobs shake silently inside my chest. "I really am so happy," I say into her shoulder.

"I know," she says.

We pull apart. She brushes my hair back from my face. "Come on," she says, "let's join the others."

She takes my hand and gives a squeeze. I feel this dream that isn't a dream anymore, these separate parts of myself coming together as one.

7

Constança invites me to join her for a weekend visit to her family's where a cousin is being married. We take the train up north and then head west on a bus. It's nearly an all day ride into the northwest region, Trás-os-Montes. Her brother-in-law meets us in the small plaza of Mirandela and drives us in a borrowed car along isolated winding dirt roads into a tiny scattering of houses. We walk a skinny footpath up to the house where Constança lived as a child.

During Constança's weekend break from her job I watch her clean, cook, and wait on her parents. She even does minor repairs on the house, trying to make up for all the time she can't be here.

Her parents appear to be in their eighties, their skin weathered like leather. Constança says her mother's fifty-eight and her father sixty-two. It's a hard life in the village, but Constança says they wouldn't trade it for anything.

Late Saturday afternoon we attend the wedding celebration held in the church with walls made hundreds of years ago from handmade bricks and stones carried from the surrounding fields. The low structure squats at the top of a knoll overlooking the little spread of village. For generations people have stood on these dirt floors, the women and girls on one side, the boys and men on the other. There are no windows or benches. The only light is cast from candles flickering in front of pictures and statues of various saints.

Everyone in the village comes to the celebration. They're dressed in traditional dark colors. The little girls of confirmation age are the only ones, besides the bride, who wear white. All of the women wear lace veils covering their foreheads. I stand with Constança in the middle of the women and girls, taking in the musty smell mixed with incense.

After the ceremony the adults walk outside with melancholy looks upon their faces while the children skip ahead to the house of the girl's parents. A variety of tables sit on the lawn with chairs scattered about.

Constança, the mother of the bride, and several aunts bring bowls and bowls of steaming soup to the long tables. People are laughing and talking and shouting. Children are scurrying among the tables, trying to find seats. The groom and a few men are standing bunched together at one of the tables, shaking hands, slapping shoulders, giving big hugs, and kissing cheeks.

As we move through several courses of the meal I watch people eat, joke, drink, and toast this couple into the long lineage of their village; marriage is an old tradition of their belonging. My thoughts drift to Helena, her arms wrapped around me the other night, her firm breasts pressed against mine. I feel the hot pleasure of wanting her, even though I promised myself not to feel this way. How can I know what she feels? Maybe she has been flirting with me or maybe I'm letting desire run away with my rational mind. Even if Helena and I had the possibility of becoming lovers it wouldn't be within this continuity of family and friends, the very thing that is so much a part of my Portuguese experience. We would be a relation without naming — invisible, a people without a language. I can't live that way.

When the fourth course arrives, croquettes of cod, rice, and sliced tomatoes and onions in vinegar and olive oil, I take up the fresh glass of white wine and make a private toast to my own questions.

Sunday morning I wake to a hangover and stomachache, wishing I had been more moderate with drink and food and thoughts. Constança asks me to join them for mass. I never go to church, but this will be a cultural experience rather than a religious one.

A half hour later Constança and her parents are dressed in black and I'm in a subdued deep blue outfit Joana has loaned me. I never wear dresses, and

88

the pumps are like remembering an old obstacle course. I got by yesterday with a pair of tan dress slacks and a frilly blouse. The village people knew I was a foreigner as soon as I exited the car so the scandal of slacks in the church had been overlooked, but two days in a row would be risking insult.

I stumble along the dirt path until we reach the house of the bride's parents where the newly married couple will be living. There I'm brought to a complete standstill.

As people walk by towards church the young husband leans out the window and unfurls a bed sheet, loudly proclaiming that the blood spot shows it was he and only he who had first claimed the virginity of his new bride, the bed sheet a banner of his possession.

The passing women blush and turn away while the men shout comments of honor to the boy in the window. And I, in a sudden confusion, begin to wonder: what is this Portugal to me?

* * * * *

I pace the living room, describing to Joana and Miguel the boy with the bed sheet. Joana watches me pacing while Miguel continues sketching on a large sketch pad in his lap.

"No one else seemed to mind that public display," I say. "I was so furious but I couldn't do anything. I mean, what could I do? Start screaming? That's what I wanted to do." I stop pacing and slump down into one of the fat chairs.

"What did Constança say?" Joana asks.

"Nothing. We continued on to church like everyone else. What the boy did was completely acceptable."

"That's the way life is in the villages," Miguel says matter-of-factly as he continues bent over the sketch pad.

I jump out of the chair and resume pacing.

"It's not just in the villages," Joana adds. "Many men I work with behave in similar fashion with their own refined concept of ownership."

"So now all men are wrong," Miguel says as he looks across at Joana, "and I'm the one guy who has to hear this feminist tirade."

"Am I lecturing you?" Joana asks sharply. "Haven't you and I always strived for openness, for something different than that kind of possessiveness? Miguel, don't you find that boy's action offensive?"

"It was rather vulgar," Miguel says, "but don't gang up on me about it."

"Who's attacking you, Miguel?" Joana says with surprise in her voice.

"I don't want to take the blame for how you two feel about men." He swiftly closes his sketch pad and stands.

"Miguel, stop being silly," Joana says as he walks towards the stairs. He looks at me out of the corner of his eye as he passes.

"Miguel, don't be angry," I say.

"I'm not," he replies curtly as he goes down the stairs into the kitchen.

I cross the living room and sit in the chair across from Joana.

"Leslie, there's going to be times when it doesn't

work well between people, when differences are jarring," Joana says.

"I'm sorry Miguel's upset."

"I'm not talking about him. He's just being bull-headed," Joana says. "I'm talking about your experience in the village."

"I don't know how to get this all together," I say, a tear rolling down my cheek.

"I don't know what you mean," Joana says.

"There's my life in the States and my friendship with you and this group of artists in Portugal. There's Helena encouraging me to get involved with her work in the villages. I feel torn in so many directions. And it really bothers me to see all this American influence here."

"Leslie, maybe you need to stop fighting it so much," Joana says. "I think you're trying to find a solution to something there's no solution for except living your life."

"Maybe I think too much about all of this."

Miguel appears in the doorway and jingles the change in his pants pocket. "Let's go out for coffee," he says.

Five minutes later we're driving fast through the night. Leave it behind, I say to myself. For now, leave all this thinking behind.

* * * * *

For days we occupy the studio. Joana and Helena draw and paint nonstop whenever they're here. Isabel comes by to add her own contribution, determined to get a young perspective in the show. Miguel always returns to the same paper tacked on an easel, where he carefully adds minute lines to an elaborate drawing that is filling up with faces. So far I see Joana, a sensual glow in her cheeks; Paulo, a mischievous glint in his eye; Teresa, a simple straightforward look; Alexandra, suave with her flawless features; Tiago, aristocratic; Helena, flashy in a large floppy yellow hat; and me, looking perplexed.

This Saturday Joana and Miguel decide to leave early for a few errands. That leaves Helena and me alone in the studio for an afternoon. After lunch we sprawl on large pillows on the floor.

"Helena, I've been wanting to talk to you about something," I jump in before I have a chance to chicken out. There's a strong pull of fear and excitement in my chest as I watch the afternoon light dancing in her clear eyes.

I've said something out loud and there's no turning back or running away or pretending I don't have feelings for this woman. I don't have to say everything today, but I can start by being open about who I truly am.

"Helena, we haven't known each other very long, but I feel like we've gotten close and become good friends. I want to be open with you about my life, but I'm a little nervous."

"I think I know what you want to tell me," Helena says.

My heart does a double somersault inside my chest. "What if I tell you and it's not what you thought and you get upset with me?"

"Be brave and try me," Helena says.

"I'm a lesbian." No longer hidden or protected, the words hang alone in the air.

"I already knew," Helena says in an even tone.

"How did you know?" I ask, relieved that she doesn't seem shaken.

"Joana told me soon after we first met. You'd just left for America after your last visit and she had the blues and needed to talk about it. She misses you terribly when you're gone. So when she talked about you that's one of the things she mentioned because she said you had just told her. She wondered about her own strong feelings for you."

"What did you say to her?" I ask, comfortable with Helena's easy attitude.

"I told her she was lucky to have such an intense friendship with a woman and not to worry about it. It made me want to know her better because I saw how deeply she felt and how much she valued your friendship."

"So you've known about me since we first met — and here I was afraid you'd reject me if you knew."

"I wouldn't reject you."

"It's been done before."

"I know, Leslie. You see, I've been involved with women too."

"Amazing!" I say in English, reaching across the pillows to grasp her hand.

She leans over and kisses our entwined fingers. I want to wrap both of my arms around her and kiss her neck, but I don't want to be foolish and rush headlong where an invitation hasn't been extended. Coming out doesn't mean she's attracted to me.

We let go and both sit up at the same time. She looks at me shyly. "We have this in common," she says.

"How is it here for you?" I ask.

"Like you, I have to travel outside of my country to keep myself sane. I can't be open here. I don't know any Portuguese women like myself and so I go to England as often as possible. It was during my studies in England that I was involved with a woman."

"Do you know any other lesbians in Portugal?"

"I don't think I would use that term," Helena says.

"You mean lesbian?"

"I don't really like to call myself anything."

"But that keeps you invisible," I say.

"I don't really want to be open in my country. But still I was pleased when Joana said you were coming, maybe even to stay. Sometimes I feel lonely not having someone to talk to about my feelings. I mean António and Susana know and they are very supportive of me, but it's not the same as it feels with you."

"Why did you come back to Portugal?" I ask.

"I planned on staying in England after my studies, but when my relationship there didn't work out I came back home."

"How long were you involved?"

"A year. Enough time for me to establish some good friends who always put me up when I go to visit. It was difficult when I first came back to Portugal. I talked to António right away, told him what I was going through. We've always been supportive of each other. But it was only after I talked with Joana that I really felt better."

"I asked Joana if she knew anyone," I say, surprised, "but she didn't tell me about you."

"Leslie, it wouldn't be her place."

"You're right," I say, still with a little knot of betrayal in my stomach. She could have at least hinted — but then the real betrayal would have been towards Helena. Joana couldn't tell me. That's the tragedy of being invisible.

"When I returned from a visit to England a couple of years ago I was really depressed for a time," Helena says. "I felt so isolated. And Joana asked me what was going on. I tried not to answer, but she kept after me for a couple of weeks, gently prodding. You know how she is." Helena looks up and we smile at each other in common appreciation.

"Anyway, I remembered all of her stories about you and it was evident she didn't walk away when you told her about yourself, so the third week when she asked me what was wrong I told her."

"How come it took so long for us to tell each other?" I ask, wondering at my own fears that kept me silent.

"We needed time to deepen our trust," Helena says.

8

As I apply glue to the stamps and place them onto several envelopes, the sticky brownish glue smears onto my fingers and across the paper. I never can get the stamps on right, always imagining the letters sticking permanently to the inside of the mail chute.

The post office is full and several people are waiting in line for the glue stick, so I return it to the small pot and push my envelopes to the far corner of the table. As I try hopelessly to clean my sticky fingertips a village man approaches me, takes off his black fedora, and asks with great politeness if I might help him. He has a form that must be filled out for the post office, but he can neither write nor read. Could I help him? He would pay me. I feel a strange sense of shame that it is I, a foreigner, who has the power to interpret for him a language rightfully his.

I stumble through the form, not quite certain myself of its exact purpose. I discover where he is to sign. I write in his address and check the appropriate boxes. When he takes the card back he again makes an offer to pay me. "Sometime you will help someone else," I say. "That is how we pass it on."

I drop my letters into the mail chute and exit the building. I cross the street and slowly walk the length of the promenade where a little boy chases after a flutter of birds and an old woman softly calls out his name.

* * * * *

I join Helena for an evening meeting in the village of Madrugada where she and a couple of friends are helping people set up marketing cooperatives for their wine and crafts. We meet in the church with a dozen women and men and talk about the concerns of their village — the lack of medical care, poor transportation into the city, the need for good roads and better education for their kids. They're already planning construction of a simple system to pipe water from the river up into the village square. I think about the thousands of times I turn on a faucet without a second thought, while these people carry their entire water supply in ceramic pitchers up a steep rocky hill.

As the conversation turns to the cooperatives Helena asks several people to present their reports. The story from one young woman particularly interests me as she describes people in a neighboring village who are learning to read and write using the educational method developed by the Brazilian, Paulo Freire.

She says with enthusiasm, "These men and women learn to read and write in three months' time. Dona Helena, we need to learn this too or we will never be able to run our own cooperatives."

Helena agrees and takes down the information, saying she's heard about Paulo Freire and would like to see how his system works.

When the meeting breaks, and people walk off into the night, Helena and I are escorted to her car by a man and woman who explain that some of the people didn't come tonight because someone was saying Helena and her friends are communists and all of this talk will only lead to trouble.

Helena asks, "What do you think?"

The man says, "I'm interested in what's going to help me do my work."

On the ride back into Coimbra Helena talks about the huge discrepancies between life in the villages and the cities, between the educated and those too poor for the luxury of literacy.

I think about the privilege of my own educated silence and begin to realize why Helena frequently talks about my need to get involved. I begin to see the wider passion that fuels her creativity, both in her painting and in her work in the village, this desire to translate experience into a form that communicates beyond the moment of experience.

"That's what knowledge is about," Helena says. "Not facts accumulated inside somebody's head, but awareness that helps us make conscious choices. I've heard this is the basis of Freire's method."

"I'm familiar with his work."

"You used his method before?" she asks excitedly.

"With the Grupo de Animação," I say. "Unfortunately it was during the fascist government and our efforts were broken when a couple of the organizers were detained in prison for several months."

"The government purposefully discouraged literacy," Helena says. "They wanted people docile and ignorant."

"It was good tonight to hear people talk clearly about their lives," I say, "and to see the efforts they're making. Their concerns are so basic and it seems obvious what needs to be done."

"It doesn't feel easy to them," Helena says. "They get called names and are gossiped about by those who don't want to organize. They feel intimidated in dealing with people with more education, like government officials and school teachers. They have doubts about succeeding." She asks, "Would you consider working with me in the village?"

"I sat through that meeting thinking of all the reasons not to get involved. I had quite a nice list till that tall skinny woman sitting next to you started talking about her fears. I mean, here I am from the States and she's from this little village and we're both adding up our justifications for inaction. The

99

difference is she's chosen to stop feeling powerless and to do something. So, yes, it's time for me to take some action too."

"Wonderful," Helena says as we cross the River Mondego and take the street to Helena's apartment.

Helena pours wine into two glasses and with a feathery touch of her hand on my arm she leads us to the couch.

"Cheers to your decision," Helena says as we click glasses and drink the slightly dry white wine.

"You've helped me rebuild some courage," I say.

"It comes from within," Helena replies.

"Inviting me to take part was helpful." I look at Helena sitting beside me and feel shy and thankful for our friendship.

We sit quietly for a moment. She touches my hand and slowly wraps her fingers into mine. I breathe shallow, thrilled and afraid. When I turn towards her our lips meet, at first cautiously then with a full smooth easiness. When we part my hands tremble.

"Helena." I lightly run my fingers back and forth across her outstretched palm. "Helena, we need to talk."

"Not now," she says.

"What if I don't stay? What if I return to the States?"

"Don't you want to be with me?" Her chestnut-brown eyes meet mine. She leans down and places a kiss on the curve of my neck and I flush with pleasure.

I run my fingers into her auburn curls and whisper close to her ear, "I want you."

Our lips meet. Hot fire builds in my stomach. Her

hand caresses the back of my neck and resistance is a quickly fading memory.

"Will you stay with me tonight?" she asks.

"Yes," I manage.

Helena caresses my cheek with her warm hand. When we kiss I love the slick motion of our lips and the lavender smell of her skin. I touch her shoulder, her arm, the edge of her hip, wanting to undress her. Her fingers run back and forth at the edge of my collar and then lightly graze across my blouse, stroking the edge of my breast. Hot air rushes my lungs. Through my clothes she massages my breasts and stomach. I arch back against the couch, yearning for her full hands on my bare skin. I watch her watching me, her brown eyes full of light.

I lean forward and slowly unbutton her blouse with a sure confidence. I pull the blouse off her shoulders and lean forward, placing my lips on the plane of her chest between collarbone and the rise of her breast, savoring the taste of her skin.

I try to unhook her bra, but fumble when I find no snap. Our eyes meet and she smiles, reaching her lips to mine, mango luscious. She pulls back from me and touches the front of her bra where she unsnaps the elastic band. Her smile and eyes are an open invitation as my hands cup her large breasts.

I sigh, my lips touching the edge of one brown nipple.

Helena moans and leans back against the couch, her arms pulling me with her. I take her nipple into my mouth and suck. Her hands tangle into my hair. Her whole body shakes loose a slight tension and she relaxes fully into the slow rhythm of my mouth.

"Querida," she says from a deep place in her throat, laying her head on the back of the couch.

I kiss across Helena's chest to her neck and up to her ear. She places her cheek alongside mine. "Leslie," she says against my skin.

She places one hand firmly on the back of my neck. The other, up under my shirt, sketches a pleasurable chill with feather light touches.

I place my hand under her skirt and massage her thigh. She whispers a hot cadence of Portuguese against my cheek. The melody of the language caresses a place in my heart as wide as the ocean.

"Helena," I whisper.

She kisses me and pulls back to reach my eyes with hers, Fourth of July sparklers in a rich deep darkness of night. We stand up long enough to find our way to the bed.

Slowly removing each piece of clothing in an endless ritual, we touch, caress, lick, massage, suck, and kiss for hours. When my hand grazes between her thighs Helena's breath catches in her throat. She holds he hips slightly off the mattress. My fingers enter her and, oh, the ecstasy in her voice.

"Minha querida namorada," she whispers, her hips rising and falling and rising, my skin silvery with the Portuguese words.

"Querida," she says. "Leslie." Her hips pause for a moment, and then she pushes higher against my fingertips, a slight quiver in her pelvis, her breath coming in short gasps.

"Oh meu deus," a quick whisper. "Oh, oh." And then a long, very long, pleasing moan.

She collapses next to me and wraps her legs and arms around my body. We breathe into the pounding of our hearts. We slow into a quieter pace, drift in and out of a light sleep, then to deeper sleep and our own separate dreams.

* * * * *

It seems very early as the phone rings and Helena pulls herself out of the tangle of sheets. I listen to her speaking in the next room, the jumble of words momentarily incoherent as I realize I've just woken out of a dream in English.

Helena steps back into the room, her naked body a pleasant shock that jolts me full awake and pulls me up to a sitting position.

"Olá," I say.

"Bom dia." She leans over to kiss me full and strong on the lips, her breasts touching warm against my chest. "That was Joana. They're coming by soon."

She sits on the bed, a slight smile on the very edge of her mouth, her direct gaze turning briefly downward in a gesture of shyness. "Leslie," she says, leaning against my naked body. "Last night was the first time I ever made love in my own country."

I wrap my arms around Helena and hold her tight against me, trying to ward off the tremendous limits of her life in Portugal. I kiss her neck and bury my face into her curly auburn hair. A moment later she pulls away and flings the covers off me. "Come on. They'll be here in forty-five minutes."

We scamper for the shower and soap each other, kissing faces through the cascade of water. With pleasure I touch Helena's full breasts and strong arms. She responds with a beautiful smile.

As the hot water turns lukewarm I wonder, What will Joana and Miguel know?

* * * * *

"Where's Miguel?" Helena asks when Joana pulls up in her car alone.

"Decided he couldn't spare the time today," Joana says, leaning out the car window. "Come on, I have some good news for you." She motions us into the car.

But Joana won't tell us the news. Instead she sits regally in the front seat and points out the sights. "For your edification," she says.

Finally we find a small café on the ocean, jutting over rocks above the wild and crashing water. The distant blue gray horizon is filled with a mass of dark clouds that threaten storm. Closer to shore the sun dances across the silver-blue surface. We sit in wobbly wrought iron chairs around a small marble-top table and view the wide horizon through tall windows. Most of the tables are filled with young couples talking and drinking coffee. The waiter leans against the bar and slowly drags on a cigarette, coolly eyeing the patrons. Joana summons him and places our order for beer and cheese sandwiches.

Helena says, "So, what's the news?"

"Yesterday afternoon," Joana explains, "I received a phone call from a German man who has businesses in Porto and Lisbon. He's interested in our exhibit and asked lots of questions. He seemed very impressed by the diversity of artists we plan to exhibit."

"How many people have submitted work?" Helena

asks quickly, leaning her elbows onto the table and looking intently at Joana.

"Thirty!" Joana says, "and as word spreads more people want to contribute."

"We're making a big step in a new direction," Helena says. She sits back in her chair as the waiter serves our beer and food.

"What's so new about it?" I ask.

"The show's wide open," Joana says. "Past exhibits have been limited and selective, excluding a lot of good artists."

"Do you think people are beginning to realize there actually are artists working in this country?" Helena bites into her sandwich.

"That's exactly what they talked about in the paper today," Joana says.

"We made the paper?" Helena asks excitedly.

"Yes. Haven't you seen it this morning?" Joana looks confused, and I wonder if Helena is so punctual on newspaper reading that this is our giveaway.

"I haven't read it yet," Helena says. She steals a quick glance at me while trying to cover a smile.

"It seems the man who called has some money contacts," Joana explains, taking the conversation back to its original source. "They want to discuss the possibility of funding a major work, possibly a book with a large visual layout or maybe a film documentation of the exhibit itself and some of the artists."

"That's fantastic!" Helena exclaims.

"Some of the people who snubbed us before are now trying to figure out how to be a part of this," Joana gloats. "Our phone has been ringing all morning."

"It's amazing," I say, "how something can get around so fast and, after just one night, cause such a widespread stir."

"That's the advantage of a small country," Helena says.

When we finish the sandwiches Helena calls the waiter to the table and orders espresso and croissants. As I listen to the machine behind the bar hiss the dark liquid into little cups I think about Miguel and wonder if his absence today confirms a growing distance I feel between us.

9

I skip up the front steps, feeling light and heady from a night of lovemaking with Helena. Helena, with whom I move past these unnecessary barriers, joining my American mind and my Portuguese heart, feeling the power of passion that speaks ideas, that creates art, that knows the sensual movement of bodies in naked dance.

I see a letter through the glass of the mailbox and fish it out. It brakes my thoughts to a quick halt. A letter from Deirdre. Just what I don't want. Why would she write after nearly half a year of silence?

It's not fair. Just when I feel I've resolved her treatment of me, she comes around again to stir up my feelings. I'm surprised at how quickly my resentment and anger rush to the forefront.

I take a few steps back and try to remember my determined self of a few minutes ago. I'm not going into a tailspin with this letter. I stuff the envelope into my pocket and decide to wait until the right time to read it, whenever the right time would be.

* * * * *

Helena and I park the car in a shady tree-lined parking lot. She pulls out a handbag containing her sketch pad, markers, and charcoal. We walk alongside a congregation of French-speaking tourists who have descended from a bus. Their heads are covered with sun hats of a variety of colors and shapes. Each person clutches an assortment of rosaries, brochures and cameras. The guide points out the low stone building we're walking past, but I don't understand anything he says.

"What is that building?" I ask Helena.

"You don't remember?" she asks. "Come on. You have to see."

We duck our heads to enter into one of the many open doorways. Inside the small dank room that smells of too many tired bodies I'm shocked into remembering. On every inch of the walls and ceiling hang creamy white plastic replicas of arms and legs and little babies. Hundreds of them hang in row upon row, the white legs all to one side, the arms to the other, and the babies tied in little bunches suspended from above. On the floor a wooden stand is crowded

108

with hundreds of white candles and strings of rosaries.

"Jesus," I mumble.

"What would the Senhoras wish to buy?" An old man steps out of the dark corner. Wrinkles crease every inch of his hands and face.

"We're only looking," Helena says as she turns to go.

The man's shaking hand reaches for her shoulder. "Don't you wish to offer prayers or thanks at the Shrine of Our Lady of Fátima?"

"No. We are only looking," Helena says as she twists away from his grasp and we both step back out into the sun.

The man comes as far as the doorway. "You aren't a tourist," he says to Helena. "You are Portuguese. Why won't you buy from me? I know you're going to the next booth." He shakes a finger towards us. "You should buy from me. I'm an old man."

"No, really, Senhor, I have come only to sketch. I'm an artist." Helena holds out her bag for him to see the pad of paper sticking up above the tan colored woven cloth.

He brushes her gesture away and calls to a couple who are walking on the path from the parking lot. "Senhor. Senhora."

We turn away and head towards the wide plaza and the Basilica. Ahead of us walk a woman and a man of about our age. Both are dressed in black, he in a worn jacket, baggy pants and a beret, she in a shirtwaist dress with a shawl over her shoulders. They carry between them, on a red string, one of the plastic babies.

109

Helena whispers into my ear, "They probably can't conceive or maybe a baby has died. They'll light a candle, say some prayers, and leave that in one of the little chapels." She motions towards the plastic replica gently swinging back and forth between them as they walk.

At the plaza the couple joins other people who are standing about or kneeling. One woman with a large beefy face and large hands rocks back and forth on her knees, frantically fingering the brown beads of her rosary. Her lips move rapidly and silently along the familiar incantations learned in childhood.

I stand on the grassy border of the huge asphalt plaza and watch in awe as the young woman we walked behind kneels down and slowly begins to move on her knees across the asphalt towards the massive stone Basilica half a mile away. The man walks beside her. A tourist with long blonde hair stands several paces in front of them and focuses his camera in their direction.

Helena finds a shady spot under a tree and makes herself comfortable with pad and pen. I wander around the low stone buildings and around the far edges of the huge plaza, watching people in various postures of supplication. I keep a distance between me and the Basilica.

"Don't you want to see the inside?" Helena asks, motioning towards the church. "I thought I might use some of the statues for drawing."

"No. I've been before," I say casually, trying to deny my fascination with the alluring pull Fátima has over people.

"You never can go enough. There's always

something new to see. The whole areas is rich in visual images."

"Even in your drawing you like to work with villagers," I say.

"This is part of my heritage." She encompasses our surroundings with a circular sweep of her hand. "All of this mysticism."

"I don't know what I believe anymore," I say.

"Were you ever religious?"

"Not like this. I had a certain focus, a kind of determination. But the Basilica frightens me with its massive tradition."

"I take comfort here," Helena says.

"Maybe I wish I could be comforted."

"You can," she says, "even if you don't believe as they do."

We look at the groups milling on the grass and happily setting out picnics, or moving towards the stone church in slow painful procession with solemn faces.

"My desire for comfort feels like a wish to escape change," I say. "I think I'm at a stage of needing agitation to grow."

From Fátima we head west to spend the weekend at the shore. Helena's cousin has loaned us the use of his cottage near the beach. I'm looking forward to two uninterrupted days. I'm not accustomed to planning so much around the moves of so many other people while relating in such an invisible fashion. It's horrible not being able to tell anyone.

We can't see the ocean from the house, but through the open windows I take in the salty smell. This is a small community of weather-worn houses with low fences of wood or brick dividing off the sandy plots of yard. Ours is the only car on the narrow lane, and the other houses seem shuttered. Maybe we'll have the whole shoreline to ourselves. Such luxury!

After opening the house we head out towards the beach. Climbing the sand dune at the end of the road we are greeted by a slight breeze off the spectacular wide ocean. We head across the bright white sand to the water's edge.

We walk the beach slowly for the longest time, Helena bending now and then to collect the tiny shells called kisses. I look at the horizon and think about Provincetown and the first summer Deirdre and I moved there and the enormous freedom we felt watching gay men and lesbians stroll up and down the street, a visible majority. Friends told us to ask the park rangers to point out the gay beach. As we pulled up to the entrance station we laughed. How could we possibly ask that so openly? When the ranger leaned into the car window we saw her pinkie ring with a double women's symbol and felt a sudden rush of being in a world of our own making.

Neither of us had lived by the ocean and it took us weeks to adjust to the wide horizon and the constantly moving water. Gradually we settled into a rhythm charted by the changing moon and the shifting tides. It was a good summer with our evening work at restaurant jobs and luxurious days in the sun.

I guess there was a time when it was good between us. My anger at Deirdre's recent silence has held off the fond memories which now begin to awaken as I walk this deserted beach with Helena. Is it because of a new lover that I'm able to let go of the past? Or is it time and distance that bring this first sign of resolution? I look out at water which has moved to shore for millions of years. My short history, though dramatic for me, is smaller than a speck in that continuum.

"You know, Helena, when I look at that water stretched between your country and mine I can't even imagine how massive it is and the variety of life it holds. It helps me trust that life is much larger than any one of us."

"Do you think the earth can survive human aggression?" Helena asks.

"My deepest hope is nature will outlast people's destructive power. I guess that's my nameless belief for which I have no tradition."

"Something to sustain you," Helena says. She takes my hand and turns us around to retrace our path along the shore. Though the incoming tide has erased our footprints, we walk with a sure confidence in our destination.

"I've felt lost for several years," I say as Helena cuddles close to me. "Knowing you is helping me come home to myself again."

"How is that?" she asks.

"You life challenges me. I want to thank you," I whisper into her ear, "for pushing me about working in the village." Helena hugs me tight. "And for taking the chance of touching me that first time." I lean back and look into her eyes.

"You encourage me too," Helena says. "You're so comfortable about loving women."

"I've had a lot of support," I say. "I'm starting to miss lesbian dances and lesbian events, places you can go and be with other women."

"Will it ever be that open here?" Helena asks.

"Hopefully, as women become more courageous to live their lives. Like the artists who want to show their work and the villagers who want literacy — all of us want the possibility to express ourselves."

"It's scary to think about living so openly."

"People have to start somewhere or nothing will ever change," I say. "There have got to be other women out there."

"I have no idea how to make contact," Helena says. "They're probably young and at the university. Even if I tried maybe I wouldn't fit in."

"Why haven't you ever just stayed in England? It must be easier there for you."

"You know how it is," Helena says, "there's a part of you that's always pulled by the country of your birth. What's it like for you?"

"I'm torn. The culture here has an intimacy I can't find in the States. Maybe I'll never find it there." I wrap my hand into Helena's and hold our hands close to my heart. I think about Provincetown where crowds of gay people set the norm, and about Portugal where only on a deserted beach can we feel the freedom to touch. "I have this constant struggle because I can live with an open heart here, but I can't live openly as a lesbian."

"I know what you mean!" Helena says.

She looks up and down the beach and then quickly kisses me on the lips. As she pulls away I lean forward and place my lips on hers for a long sensual kiss. She pulls back, looks over her shoulder, and starts us off again at a brisk pace down the beach.

"Do you have a lover in the States?" Helena asks.

"For two years I was with Deirdre. We talked about buying land together and building a house. We went to a tourist resort to make fast money, but things fell apart."

"What happened?" Helena asks.

"Deirdre liked all the options."

"What do you mean?"

"Provincetown's a gay resort and our first summer we had a lot of fun watching all the new women come through town. There are so many lesbians! I mean, the main street is wall-to-wall gay people every hour of the day in the summertime."

"I can't imagine!" Helena says. "I wish I could see that!"

"In the winter, when the cold comes, almost everything closes down and the tourists leave. Then in the spring you go through two-and-a-half months of the shops, restaurants, and bars slowly reopening. As each place opens there's a party and everyone comes out of hibernation for champagne and great spreads of food. Then the tourists begin to come back."

"It sounds wonderful," Helena says.

"Unfortunately for me Deirdre decided she wanted access to that wide selection of women. By April she was having a new affair every weekend and doing cocaine. She went through her share of the savings for our house. I made a lot of excuses about what was happening, but by June we had separate apartments and separate bank accounts. I saw her sometimes on the street with another woman, usually

115

wired on coke. She never talked to me again. Even when she moved out of town she didn't look me up."

"That's terrible," Helena says. "How could she change so suddenly?"

"Maybe she was always that way and I wouldn't see the real person as long as it was safe between us," I say, surprising myself with the burden that lifts off me. She's one person, not my whole identity.

"Sometimes I think I would like to meet other Portuguese women like myself," Helena says.

"Maybe we could check out things in Lisbon," I say.

We continue on in silence until we reach the cottage door, where we enter into a full two days of doing what we want. It seems both luxuriously long and much too short.

* * * * *

Dinner at Joana and Miguel's is the usual ruckus with everyone talking at once. I'd gotten accustomed to quiet evenings with Helena.

"Are you and Helena thinking about living together?" Cristina asks.

"Oh no," I say, feeling immediately uncomfortable. "She doesn't really have the space. We've just been . . ." I falter about for an explanation.

"Getting to know each other," Miguel says, finishing my sentence with a cool look across the table.

"I'm asking around for students with whom you can share a place," Cristina says. "If you're still interested."

"Yes. Thanks, Cristina." I try to sound cheerful to offset the growing unease I feel with Miguel.

After dinner I sit in the kitchen with Constança as she eats her meal. I don't want to stay in the same room with Miguel as he broods over the newspaper. I help Constança load the dishwasher. We talk about her night school studies and about the handsome priest who directs the choir group where she goes each Thursday night.

"How can such a young man give up marriage and family?" she asks.

I think about Constança's life, working for others since the age of twelve. She'll probably do this work her entire life, possibly much longer than the priest.

She asks me various questions about America and I wonder how I can describe a place so foreign to her experience. I think this until Constança sits in a chair at the kitchen doorway, to watch the latest American TV serial that Miguel has turned on. I see it is not the ocean that limits a proper explanation, but this tidal wave of fabricated stories.

I drift around the room aimlessly, moving from chair to chair, flipping through a photo album, looking at Joana's newest painting she's just hung, glancing at the faces glued to the TV. Finally I go to my room and grab up the book by my bed, wondering if I'm in the mood to read. I open the pages to where the letter from Deirdre serves as a marker. My anger and sadness are sparked again by the sight of her handwriting, and then the choice of her words.

Dear Leslie.

I start to cry, crumple up the page and throw it against the wall in the corner. After a minute I think, girl, do you really feel this or are you making up some kind of drama? I retrieve the letter, flatten it out on the desk, and lean over the crinkled words.

Ok, even I mess up sometimes, she writes, her sentence a familiar joke that isn't funny anymore.

I just had to split for awhile. Had to get away. Had to take my space. I'm sure you understand. Sarah tells me you've decided to continue on there for awhile. Well, maybe we'll run into each other someday at the Michigan Festival. See you.

Deirdre

As usual, Deirdre's used her perfunctory style of not dealing. Why should I have expected anything else? The biggest surprise is my calm response. My silent struggle of the past several months is released with written words that now seem so small, so unconnected. I try to make myself cry, but no tears are there.

10

Joana motions me to join her on the living room couch while she finishes writing a letter. I enjoy the quiet in the house and the warmth of the morning sun slanting through the windows.

"Planning this art exhibit is really helping my work," Joana says as she folds the letter and slides it into an envelope. "I feel more productive than I have in a long time."

"Can I see what you have there?" I ask, pointing to the large sketch pad that she works on in the house.

Joana pulls it protectively against her chest. "It's a bit more private. I'm sure I won't enter any of this in the show."

"Would you prefer I not see it?"

"Of course I don't mind. I'm just shy about it. Let's get some coffee first." She jumps up and heads for the kitchen. I follow.

"Cristina really likes the English speaking discussion group," Joana says.

"It's a lot of fun." I place two cloth napkins on the tray.

"Cristina says it's helping the students in their classes." Joana pops a piece of cheese into her mouth.

"Yes, and I'm making enough money to start looking for a place of my own."

Joana turns quickly towards me and places her hands on her wide hips, her elbows out at right angles. "I've gotten accustomed to you being here," she says. "It's different when you're in the house. You add a new dimension to our family." Joana picks up the tray and I follow behind with the coffeepot, thinking how fortunate I am to have such friends in my life.

Instead of heading for the living room, where the sketch pad waits, Joana leads us to the dining room table. I know we're traveling this morning at Portuguese time instead of American, with directness and rapidity replaced by poetic and gentle movement.

We drink coffee and look at photographs of travels to Italy and Greece. The architecture is incredible. I tell Joana about the ancient animal-shaped mounds left by Native Americans in the Midwest and the housing carved into stone in the West. She's fascinated by the Native American use of land as ritual and art.

"I think the biggest challenge," she says, "is trying to express great mysteries on canvas. Miguel and I have been together for twenty years and we still have days when we wake up to find a great surprise in each other."

"That's more than a lot of people can say. It seems the greatest course is boredom, something many people suffer."

"The first year you left I was bored and depressed for a long time." Joana stares blankly at the photo album and touches its edges with a nervous hand.

"Why didn't you say anything?"

"Because it wouldn't have brought you back." She closes the album and places her hand on the dark leather cover with a gesture of finality. "Every time you come for a visit I have to make an adjustment afterwards. I hope you never go back. But who knows, maybe now we'll become complacent in our friendship." She gives me a quick shy glance and then returns her gaze to the dark leather cover.

"I can't imagine that," I say.

"I hope not," Joana says. "You know, I've never had the intensity of friendship with anyone like I have with you, except for Miguel."

"But it's Portugal which offers that intensity," I say.

"No. You can't know how different it is when you're not here. What you don't see is the immensity you bring to our lives."

"I never thought about it," I say.

"You've always been aware of the great

importance my culture plays in your life. But you've also opened us to many things. Would you like to see my sketches now?"

"Sure."

"Let's go to the Jardim Botânico where we won't be disturbed."

Joana grabs the pad and we head out for the street. Outside the door Joana turns right, choosing the longer walk to the Jardim.

At the top of the hill we stop to catch our breath and look behind us at the row of two story houses and low stone walls we have passed.

"You know," she says, "I'm not always as free as I seem."

"What do you mean?" I ask.

Joana and I look out past the town at the blue gray flat land stretching in the distance.

"When you first told me you were a lesbian I wanted it to be a phase you were going through. Even though I knew it wasn't."

"Why?" I am leading us onto the next street of two and three story stucco houses, low stone fences, and tiny yards with green shrubbery and an occasional tree.

"I guess because you'd fit in then and it'd be easier."

We walk half a block without talking, past typical homes with orange ceramic roofs, lattice iron balconies, and blue inlaid azulejos.

"It wouldn't be easier for me" finally I say. "I'm happy for who I am."

"I know. I don't know why I feel this way. It's stupid of me."

"It's what society teaches you. It keeps my life

invisible and fills your head with untrue stories. Why are you thinking about this now?" I am already tired of this talk.

"When you told me before I really didn't have to deal with it. But now, well, Miguel and I notice you and Helena are spending a lot of time together, and I know about Helena's experiences, and, well, really this isn't my business."

"Why didn't you tell me about Helena?"

"It wasn't my place."

"But I didn't know anybody. I didn't know I could ever meet anyone here!" I feel frustration pound against the underside of my skin.

"We don't talk so openly about those things in Portugal," Joana says matter-of-factly.

"Talk needs to start somewhere! Otherwise, how will anything change?"

"I didn't think I had the right. Maybe she wouldn't want you to know." Joana quickens our pace.

"You could have asked her what she thought."

"I guess I was afraid," Joana says. "She and I haven't spoken about it since that first time."

"About what?" I say.

"You know," she says.

"Just say it." My voice sounds a bit too sharp.

"What difference does it make?" she shoots back.

"Because as long as you don't say the words then I'm invisible. You're afraid aren't you?"

"I don't understand it. I don't understand how you can have feelings for a woman. I know there are homosexuals, but I don't understand how they turn out that way."

I carefully state the question I've asked a hundred

times at parties, at conferences, at lectures, "How did you become heterosexual?"

"I just am," she says.

"And I'm just gay. Why is it so frightening?"

"I don't know," Joana says, "but I do know I feel a little jealous. How can I be jealous of you and Helena?"

"Joana," I say, taking a long, deep breath to calm my anger. I look at this woman who has been a constant friend, even though time and the wide ocean could so easily have worn down that bond. I don't want ignorance and impatience to tear us apart. "Joana, you and I have a very special friendship that we can never replace."

"Do you ever feel sexual about me? Oh God, I can't believe I asked that!" She stops and pivots a full circle on one foot, her face buried in her hands. I can't tell if she's laughing or moaning.

"Haven't we both felt that at times?" I ask.

"Well, maybe . . . probably . . . I mean, I guess we have. This is definitely not comfortable to talk about."

"There's nothing right or wrong about feelings," I say.

"What do you mean?" There is a twinge of defensiveness in Joana's voice.

"Joana, you know feelings have the right to their own integrity. That's always been the base of our friendship."

"But are you saying we should be lovers or something?" Joana stops in her tracks and looks at me as she fidgets with the frayed string wrapped around her sketch pad.

"That's not what I'm talking about." I take a few steps past her.

"I guess I'm reacting a little strongly," she says, catching up with me again.

"There's nothing wrong with sexual feelings. You and I have chosen not to pursue them, that's all."

"You make it sound so simple."

"Well, Miguel doesn't seem comfortable with the situation. Maybe it would be better now if I moved out."

"Don't worry about Miguel," Joana says. "I think his male pride is hurting. It's good for him to learn that men really are not the center of the universe."

"He's reacting to what he's been taught."

"It's like we want everything to be the same," Joana says as we turn onto the tree lined garden path.

"To be well-defined and within certain boundaries."

"But I'm more open than that," Joana adds, slowing our pace to a leisurely stroll.

"So am I, but still I have my own terrors."

"Like that wide ocean," she says, "maybe it's only a barrier you've created for yourself."

I begin to run inside, down a long thin corridor, and hear the distant sound of a door shutting with a strong sharp force, followed by a great space without words — this chosen silence. I know I should listen to what she says, but I'm not ready.

"Being open is no easy task." I place each word carefully outside of the silence and following the words back down the long, thin corridor, back to the sunlight of mid-morning, back to the side of Joana and this garden path, the larger question stored inside.

"Why don't we sit down," Joana says in her regular tone, seemingly oblivious to my momentary flight. "I'll show you my sketches."

She opens the pad and slowly begins to turn through the pages. All of the drawings are nudes — women alone, women with other women or with men. In some the people are making love, in others the repose is serene, meditative.

"They're very good," I say.

"I don't know if I'll ever show them," Joana says. "I always thought I was so open, but I still have a lot to learn. If I sketch long enough maybe your life will be what I see instead of my own ignorance."

"That determination is the reason you're such a special friend." I lean over and give Joana a big hug which she returns with strong arms. And I wonder, how strong is my own determination?

* * * * *

The next morning Helena and I rise before daybreak, dressing hurriedly in the slight chill of morning. My eyes are tired and I splash water on my face to get my blood flowing faster.

We both are quiet as we drive through the dark. Twenty minutes later we pull up the stony dirt road to the church. I wonder if we've mixed up our dates as the building is a massive dark presence. I'd rather be in bed.

Just as I'm hoping the meeting has been called off and we can return to our warm covers, a stocky woman steps out from the side of the building and comes over to Helena's car window.

"The lights are off in the church," the woman says. "We don't know why, but we'll manage anyway. Please come with me and I'll show you the way."

Helena and I follow behind the woman, holding hands so as not to stumble across the uneven earth. We pass the stone bell tower and walk the backside of the building where the dark is even more complete. I can't see my hand in front of me as I reach out to touch the hard, cold stone for support and guidance. I take each step gingerly.

"Here." The woman's voice next to me makes me jump. She gropes along my side, finds my arm, and pulls me towards her. My reflex is to protect my face, but my other hand is pulling Helena behind me. I walk in blind trust where the woman leads. I can feel from the slight temperature change and a musty smell that we've probably entered the building.

"You can sit here," the woman says as her hand slides down my arm. She bends forward into the dark and I bend with her, our hands groping until we touch a wooden plank.

I finger the skinny board and guide myself in its direction, pulling Helena with my other hand. A second later she sits down half on my lap. We both giggle nervously and she slides carefully to the side. I lean back slowly until I touch a cold stone wall that instantly sends a chill through my light jacket and straight into my bones.

The voice of the woman who met us at the car comes out of the dark. "We're sorry about the lack of light. You see, most of us have known this church

127

since we were babies, so we can comfortably find our way around. Maybe by the sunrise we will be able to better introduce ourselves to you."

There's chuckling around the room and I realize all the women are already here and this is the beginning of the meeting. What a strange sensation. Not being able to see I had assumed we were alone.

The women begin to explain to us how they've been learning to read and write. Their varied voices place words into the dark damp air with confidence.

"We meet either in the morning, like today, or we meet late at night," a woman says. "There are so many other necessities to be taken care of that these are the only times we have."

"We meet sometimes just with the women," says another voice, soft like the velvet night, "because sometimes there are things to be discussed that just the women understand. At first the men got mad."

"Yes, they said next we'd throw them out of our beds!" This statement is followed by a great laughter.

"The men were afraid we would let our children go hungry," a woman sitting next to me says in a raspy tone.

"But we wanted to talk among ourselves," a deep, quivery old voice adds from across the room.

"So we decided this was necessary," someone says, "and eventually the men saw that it was not a horrible thing."

"Still, sometimes my husband asks, what do you talk about?" These words are placed cautiously, almost in a whisper.

The pause which follows feels endless without the cadence of the women's voices to mark the time. I lean back against the chill of the stone wall.

A young woman says, "Some people are afraid this work is communist."

"Others say why learn to read and write now? It is too late."

"What do you think?" Helena asks.

"It is very important! We are every age here, from sixteen years to seventy and every one of us has the desire to learn."

The sky begins to lighten a bit, showing a slight difference in the outline of a window that begins to appear. I still can't see anyone in the room, but I'm able to distinguish different voices and mark in my mind where some of the women are sitting.

"Who is your teacher?" Helena asks.

"Sister Maria. She's here with us now," one of the women says.

"Yes. We're sorry we can't show you any of our charts and writings today," Sister Maria says. "However, I'm glad you want to do literacy work. It's important for you to hear what is being learned in our village, so you can take the stories back to the people of Madrugada. Would someone like to tell her story?"

"I am forty-seven years old and I never really knew how to read," a woman says in a sing-song voice. "I had to quit school in the third grade to help my mother with the other children." She pauses and the darkness once again wraps the silence. When she speaks again, her words are placed carefully, as if each could stand on its own. "I always wanted to go back, but my father said there's no reason for a girl to learn reading and writing. It was better that I learn cooking and taking care of babies. Well, he was right until Sister Maria came and we started our weaving cooperative. Now I can earn extra money with my work. Sister Maria says we need to learn all of the things so we won't be dependent on her and we can manage our own business. That's why I'm learning to read, so I can help the cooperative run and be our own business."

After a moment of quiet the woman sitting next to me speaks. "I sure love learning to read and write," she says, "because you see my son and his family have emigrated to Switzerland and now I can write them letters and they can write to me. It is a long time between their visits. Guida," she says. "Guida, tell your story. That's my daughter over there," she says.

"Oh Mãe," a young woman pleads.

"Yes, Guida," Sister Maria says. "The Senhoras would like to hear your story."

"When I was in school," the young woman begins, "I thought I was very smart. I didn't want to sit there all day. I wanted to be outside. I wanted to earn money like my brother and his wife who went to Switzerland. I thought their life was very romantic. So I quit school and began working full-time in the field with my mother and father. But I can't leave my parents alone and go off by myself. So here I stay. I want to make life better in the village and if I improve my reading and writing maybe I can do something."

The sky continues to move from darkness to dawn. By the window I see the slight outline of the side of a woman's face. As the talking continues I watch her face take on more form and definition, the rugged and deeply tanned skin of a woman who has worked in the fields for years, probably for longer than I've lived.

I listen to the stories and feel goose bumps rise along my arms. There is truly a power in words, particularly for people who have been denied language, a power that these people are beginning to unlock.

The old woman by the window leans forward and says in a strong, deep voice, "I would say we are learning not only to read and write, but we are learning to think. If we can't think for ourselves then we always have to depend on others to translate what we should already know."

I remember the man in the post office. I think about Joana's own effort to make reality visible through her drawings, and about all the artists who are excitedly waiting to display their work. Something in all of this is calling me, but I don't yet know what it is.

As the women continue on with their stories their faces begin to rise out of the darkness with the morning sun. I travel with them, a witness to the power of words moving silence into action.

11

"Leslie, wake up," Constança says, giving my feet a shake to stir me out of a nap.

"What is it, Constança?" I rub my eyes and stretch into a sitting position on the edge of the bed.

"There's an American downstairs," she says.

Fear and excitement jump into my chest, waking me fully into consciousness.

"I don't remember the name. It's someone Senhor Doctor brought home."

Downstairs Miguel introduces me to Audrey. We shake hands and say hello. She's wearing a blue jean jacket, a tailored cotton shirt, loose fitting khaki pants, and sneakers. Her blonde hair is cut in a pageboy that loosely frames an open, inquisitive face. She looks about twenty years old.

"Audrey came into the hospital to see about donating blood," Miguel says. "I've never met anyone who wanted to donate blood, unless it was for their family."

"Are you living here?" I ask, having to speak slowly as I translate my thoughts into English.

"I'm traveling about," she says. "I was with friends in England and France. They went on to Italy, but I wanted to explore Portugal. In a week I'll meet them in Madrid."

"That's nice," I say, a bit resistent to her exuberance.

"Miguel was very kind to invite me to stay for a couple of days. He said you would recommend them for a good time."

"Oh, yes. They've shown me so much of Portugal."

"How long are you staying?" Audrey asks, returning to her seat as Miguel and I sit on the couch across from her.

"I'm not sure." I glance towards Miguel. "Well, for now, permanently."

"Really!" she says. "That's fantastic! I have to be back soon to start winter term at the university. My parents gave me a high school graduation present of six months' travel. It's been fantastic."

"I should say so."

We talk over lunch, with even Cristina and Isabel a bit more confident in their English. They like her because she's familiar with their favorite musicians.

133

She tells several animated stories about clubs she went to in England, and about fringe music groups. The girls are captivated and want to hear every detail. Zé keeps after Joana and me to translate. By the end of the meal I realize English doesn't seem so foreign and Audrey's a lot of fun.

We plan an excursion for the weekend, and a small party for Friday night.

* * * * *

Audrey and I spend the afternoon walking the streets of Coimbra. I tell her what I know about the city, a scattering of history and various points about architecture and art that I've learned from Miguel and Joana. She tells me she's from Albuquerque and she talks about what she wants to do with her life. Her voice is enthusiastic, her words hopeful.

I say, "It's been a long time since I've heard an American speak with confidence about trying to organize and bring about change." I watch her big springy strides in consistent rhythm up and down the hilly streets, her long thin arms swinging loosely.

"Well it has to be done, you know. We can't very well allow the injustices of our government to continue." She gives me an intensely serious look with her youthful blue eyes.

I try to hold my old doubts at bay, my pessimism capable of a sarcastic edge. But why do I care? Of course she reminds me of myself some years ago, standing in that exact same posture, open and ready to take on the world.

"How did you turn out this way," I ask, "when

so many others your age seem concerned only about business degrees and good paying jobs?" Even as I ask the question I feel silly, taking on the role of a person set in her ways. I'm not like this!

"Leslie, there are other people who feel the same as I do," Audrey says. "Maybe not all quite as enthusiastic. It seems folks your age are so cautious. I don't understand it."

"You know, Audrey, maybe I am too cautious with my life." I grab her hand and sprint across the cobblestone street. "Your enthusiasm is challenging my complacency."

The rest of the afternoon, as we walk, Audrey describes the work she's been doing with the Sanctuary Movement, helping refugees who've left Central America where thousands of people have died at the hands of death squads. Sarah had recently written from New York to say the Peace Coalition was considering establishing Sanctuary with some other groups in the Catskills. So there are people working in the States.

I ask, "What do your parents think about all of this?"

"You probably think my parents are rich. That's what everyone says around here. They think every American is rich and lives in Dallas."

We both start to laugh. We laugh so hard that we stop walking. I lean back against a blue-tiled building and laugh until my stomach hurts. Audrey hops up and down in front of me giggling and whooping. A middle-aged woman carrying two plastic bags heavy with groceries trudges past, her solemn face turned in a sharp angle towards us. I grab Audrey's arm and pull her next to the wall. She leans her blonde head back against a faded and torn poster announcing a political rally, her blue eyes dancing with light.

"It's fun to be silly in the streets," I say.

"And so easy to make a scene!" Audrey says.

"I used to get upset by men who followed me, whispering about the easy American girl. But then one day I just stopped in the middle of the sidewalk and told this guy to stop bothering women in the street."

"You told him just like that?"

"Yeah. And in a second everyone else stopped and wanted to know what was going on. I didn't need to say another word because everyone around me got into a heated debate, while the first guy tried to slink away from the crowd. I discovered how easy it is to get everyone involved."

"Feminism in action," Audrey says.

"Education in the streets," I say.

"That's exactly what I was going to tell you. My parents claim education is more than what you get in a classroom. That's why they encourage me to travel. How about your life? What are you doing?"

"I'm trying to figure out where to be and what to do."

"Can I ask you something?"

"Sure," I say, taking Audrey's elbow and steering her across the cobblestones. "Come on, let's go into the park. There's a nice fountain where we can sit."

"Well, I was wondering," she says, "are you a lesbian?"

"Yeah." I glance at her. "Are you?"

"No. But there's a great women's community in

Albuquerque. If you come back to the States you should consider it. We're doing good work and people are open-minded. There's some real coalition building going on."

"It feels funny to be talking like this in English." I point us towards the gray stone fountain where a trickle of water cascades into a small round pool.

"Why?" she asks.

"Because I'm crossing over a line I hadn't expected to be dealing with here."

"Maybe there aren't lines. Maybe lines are just something you need to construct for yourself." She sits on the pool's edge and dips her hand into the water.

"Wisdom out of the mouths of babes," I say.

"Don't be an ageist," she says, giving a friendly splash of water in my direction.

* * * * *

Friday night's party is a blast! Even Susana and António are here, he in his beaded hippie shirt. This is the first time they've met Joana and Miguel, and António and Miguel are already upstairs getting stoned. Miguel's never been stoned before. I find them in the bathroom like two teenagers sneaking a buzz.

The music is as eclectic as the party — jazz, pop, rock, fados — depending on who's standing by the stereo when an album is finished. When the beat is right the dining room is filled with people dancing. The table pushed back against the wall is filled with pastries and cakes and various drinks. Miguel and Joana are known for great parties. The conversations move anywhere from architecture to good political jokes to international travel to the upcoming art exhibit.

Zé and Audrey are in the corner screaming out their laughter over a board game that Zé brought from upstairs. Joana joins them while I sit in my favorite chair watching the people come and go around me, listening to the conversations shift and move.

"Come and dance," Paulo says, reaching for my hand.

By the end of the evening I'm pleasantly tired. As people begin to leave Helena whispers in my ear, "Come and spend the night with me."

I grab some clothes and we say goodnight to everyone. As the door shuts I hear Cristina ask in a bewildered voice, "Where is Leslie going?"

12

My life feels pretty regular to me. I have my resident registration and the consulate has my address. I work three days a week teaching English and once a week meet with the English discussion group at Cristina's school. I can get myself around town on the streetcars and am getting involved in literacy work with the weaving co-op in Madrugada. This is my real life, not just a tourist visit.

I have enough money to move out of Joana and Miguel's house, and a change of place may lessen Miguel's uncomfortable feelings toward me. But for some reason I'm hesitant. I think I've gotten accustomed to having dinners cooked for me every night and never having to run the vacuum cleaner. But more seriously, I think I'm not ready to make the final decision to live in Portugal. I've been on the move for too many years, living like a gypsy. After being in any apartment or house for several months I start to get an itch and usually pack up and change locations. After a year or two in any town I pull out the maps and start to investigate. My problem is I don't have a gypsy family.

I remember the first time I saw real gypsies, in Porto a few years back. One of them must have been in the hospital because a group was camped out under the trees on the hospital grounds. I walked slowly past the stone wall that separated us and looked across the grass at the gathering of women, children, and men. I wanted to stop and stare. I wanted to call out to them and invite myself over to their campsite, but I didn't. I wasn't sure what language they spoke and I'd heard stories about their stealing, incest, and violence. The children had dirty faces and their clothes looked grimy. All of this frightened me into staying on the other side of the wall. I wouldn't stop and look, but for several days I returned to walk slowly past that gathering.

Then one day, their sick companion either dead or cured, they moved on. I've always wondered what it would be like to travel with companions.

* * * * *

Miguel and Joana are in Paris for a few days

140

where Miguel is making a presentation at a medical convention sponsored by UNESCO.

Tonight, after much insistence from Isabel and myself, Constança joins us at the table for dinner. The three kids, and we two adults eat leisurely. I continually tease them as they discuss in great detail what they expect will happen tonight on their favorite TV program. Cristina brings out wine glasses and pours a small amount into each. We hold our glasses with posturing fingers and immediately take on various accents, trying to imitate the speech of rich people. Zé hops up from the table and takes the plate of codfish and rice to Constança for a second serving. Constança laughs and takes food from the platter.

When the doorbell rings Constança grabs for her plate to head for the kitchen.

"Constança, don't," I say. "I'm sure it's Helena. She said she was coming for desert."

As I reenter the room with Helena, Constança immediately rises and starts to pick up the dishes.

"Constança, you don't need to do that," I say. "Kids, would you mind clearing off the table?"

"Sure, we'll do it," Zé says.

"No," Constança says. "I'll do it."

"We'll all help," Helena says, and we each grab plates and platters and head for the kitchen.

The six of us crowd into the small room and in a couple of minutes of loud and frantic work we have the dishwasher full and everything else put away.

"Get set up for your television program," I say to Constança and the kids. "Helena and I will make a tray for tea and the cake she brought."

Isabel wraps her arms around my neck for a quick hug and then scoots out of the kitchen. I watch Cristina sulk off after her sister, closing the door behind them.

After dessert and TV the three kids go off to bed, Constança retires to her room, and Helena and I settle into the couch in the living room.

"I wish you could stay all night." I put my arm around her shoulders.

"It's not possible, so why think about it?" Helena's body is stiff under my touch.

"Because it makes me mad." I pull my arm away from her and rest my hands in my lap. "Doesn't it make you feel bad to sneak around?"

"I don't think of it like that," Helena says. "Why should it be anyone's business what we do?"

"Don't you see that being so invisible affects how you feel about yourself?" I look at the thin line of Helena's mouth set firm in a serious face, her forehead wrinkled in thought.

After a glance at me Helena pensively stares at the wall. "Leslie, this is my country. I've never been open here before."

I say, "It's hard for me to be so closed."

"That's just the way it is here," she says. "I guess I accept it because I never had anyone pushing me to think it could be different."

"Why don't we see if we can find other women here?" I turn sideways on the couch and look directly at Helena. She keeps facing forward, looking at the wall. I wrap my fingers into her hand.

"It's easy for you," she says, gently accepting my fingers. "In your country there are groups and organizations and newsletters. I don't even know how I could begin to talk to someone."

"You were open with me." I give Helena a nudge with my arm.

"You're a foreigner," she says matter-of-factly.

I look at my skin, the summer tan faded and nearly gone, my pale fingers wrapped in Helena's olive brown hand. Yes, I am the foreigner, offering some sense of freedom in my difference. I look at my flannel shirt, blue jeans, and sneakers — not exactly exotic.

"Helena," I say, "why don't we go to Lisbon, see if we can find a place where women meet?"

"I don't know," she says.

"What could it hurt to go to Lisbon?" I ask.

"Word could get around," she says. "I could lose my job, my family, everything. That's why I always go to London. It's safer for me."

"How about if I went to Lisbon and looked around? I could tell you if I find anything."

"Maybe you're right," Helena says. "It would be nice to know one or two discreet women. Not the loud kind, the macho ones —"

"You know women like that?"

"I've heard stories about bawdy women who drink too much and act like men."

"Those stories are told just to scare you," I say.

"I saw women in London like that," she contends. "Their heads were nearly shaved and they acted so tough . . ."

"Do I act like that?"

"No."

"Come here." I wrap my arm behind her back and

pull her tight against me. "Helena," I whisper into her ear.

She turns her lips to mine and we kiss. She runs her fingers lightly on the back of my neck and up into my hair.

"I could kiss you all night," I say.

"Hey, you two," Isabel says, as we jerk back away from each other, Helena jumping straight up off the couch.

"Isabel!" I say.

"Don't look so embarrassed. I know about you two and, hey, it's fine with me."

Helena slides into one of the chairs, her back to Isabel, her bent head in her hands.

"Isabel, what do you want?" I say, shaken by this revelation.

"I'm sorry to interrupt, but I forgot to ask if we're going to Paulo and Teresa's tomorrow." She looks at Helena and then at me.

"Sure, if that's what you want," I say, trying to match Isabel's casual attitude.

"That's what we want to do." Isabel bounds across the floor to give me another good night kiss. She leans over and kisses Helena on the top of her head. "Good night," she says. Helena doesn't move.

"Good night," I say.

After a minute I hear the bedroom door shut. Helena still hasn't moved. I kneel on the carpet beside her chair.

"Helena," I whisper. I see she's crying. "Helena, sweetheart. It's okay."

"She knows, Leslie."

"It's okay," I say.

"But who else knows?" She looks up through a tangle of auburn curls, her eyes skittish with fear.

"Isabel's so open," I say. "She's fine with us."

"What about those who aren't?"

I think about Cristina and wonder if we were the reason for her sulkiness this evening.

"Helena," I whisper as I bury my head in the crook of her arm. I feel her tighten and slightly pull away. I straighten up and place my hand on her forehead, coaxing her head to rise and our eyes to meet.

"Helena, do you want to be hidden your whole life?"

* * * * *

For the next two days Cristina continues to sulk around the house. I want to talk with her but I'm not sure what to say, so I give her a wide berth as she leaves for school and makes brief appearances at dinner. Isabel is her usual affectionate self and Zé seems oblivious to any tension or changes.

The day Joana and Miguel return they take the kids for a weekend visit to the family home in the interior. Constança goes to her sister's in another city, and I stay put in order to enjoy the solitude. It's been a couple of months since I've been in a house alone for more than just a few hours.

I take a long, comforting soak in the big bathtub, enjoying the absolute quiet in the huge house. I think about Helena, who's been feigning a busy schedule since the evening with Isabel. Maybe she just needs some time. And I'm confused myself. It's unhealthy

145

that she has to live her life so closed, but what options does she have? If I go back across the ocean will she be left with an openness not viable in her own country? Maybe she will live like a gypsy herself and move to England. Is this the choice we have — consciousness creating a nomadic people who move about not as a tribe but as disbanded individuals?

I put on Joana's bathrobe and go downstairs to fix myself a simple dinner of scrambled eggs and toast. I put on a jazz tape and watch the light of the sunset move through the dining room, touching everything with a light wash of pinkish blue and moving through deeper blues into black. Still I sit, reaching now and then to the cassette player to flip over the same Grover Washington tape. I can listen to him for hours, and so I do.

When I finally rise I feel centered and rested. I didn't know I'd lost contact with my inner self, but the lack of time alone had caught me up in a lot of other people's stories. I realize I have some decisions to make. I can't keep living at Joana and Miguel's indefinitely, as if waiting for life to make choices for me. And I need to make time available for Helena, to see where we go from here.

13

Susana comes by to tell me she and António have moved in together and want me to join them.

"I'll think about it," I tell her.

"How come you're hesitant?" she asks. "Maybe we should talk about it. It helps to talk things out, you know?"

We leave it at that. She gives me the address and I tell her I'll stop by soon to have a look.

* * * * *

Helena and I have seen each other only briefly since the evening Isabel found us kissing, and we haven't yet spoken about it. Tonight the two of us join Joana and Miguel for dinner at Tiago and Alexandra's.

Helena's wearing a green silk dress and dark hose with a delicate black pattern. She's cut her hair to just below her ears and the auburn curls are thick and carefree about her head. I try not to think about her dark brown eyes, the red lips that I want to kiss.

Miguel stands by the fireplace, his back to the leaping flames. As he sips liqueur he watches Helena who's listening to Tiago describe their latest acquisition, a large woven white rug.

When Tiago finishes Miguel clears his throat and gestures with his glass towards Helena. "Tiago," he says, "what do you think of Portuguese women who wait so long to marry?"

Tiago looks at Helena, a nervous smile on his lips. He looks at Miguel.

"Helena, don't you ever want to marry?" Miguel asks.

"Maybe," Helena says.

"Who will care for you in your old age if you don't have children?" Miguel pokes the glass in her direction.

"It's possible to have kids without marrying," I say in a light-hearted tone. "With the advancement of modern technology it's even possible to do it without direct assistance from a man."

Miguel shoots a dagger look in my direction, jolting me with surprise. Tiago stands up and nervously fingers his beard. "I'll see if Alexandra and Joana have dinner ready."

Miguel holds the glass to his lips. I turn to the flames dancing behind his back and watch the yellow white light move without pattern or form, like the tension in the room.

"Well, Helena," Miguel says. "I do have a colleague at work who wishes to ask you out."

My stomach plummets.

"He saw you at the party when Audrey was here."

Miguel looks at me and smiles. He knows what he's doing.

"Well, maybe," Helena says. "If I can find some time. I'm so busy with the literacy work and getting ready for the exhibit." She shifts on the couch and glances in my direction, her nervous eyes not meeting mine.

"You two seem to make time for each other," Miguel says, his voice an ice-blue chill in my ears.

I feel the air shift between us. The fire spurts and flares with the collapse of the kindling and one of the logs tumbles deeper into the flames.

Helena stands up and says in a forced casual tone, "I'm going to see how dinner is coming."

Miguel and I stare silently at each other across a gulf much wider than the actual space. Too much change is happening too fast in this stillness, maybe even something irreversible.

Joana enters the doorway, cracking the silence, "Dinner's ready."

At the table I grab a seat next to Joana and with her closeness try to calm the high vibration inside my head. Since Miguel sits on the other side of Joana we're spared any direct eye contact. Helena's across the table between Alexandra and Tiago, and is telling

149

an animated story about chicken soup. Tiago meets my eyes shyly for a moment, and I wonder, What does everyone know?

I sit quietly through the vegetable soup and the entree of squid stew and rice, listening to my friends fill the room with talk. As we finish our second helpings Joana leans close to me and says in a low voice, "You're very quiet tonight, Leslie."

"Sometimes I am," I say, thinking about Miguel's anger and hoping Joana won't ask me to explain my silence.

Alexandra puts her hand lightly on my shoulder and leans across the table to pick up the large ceramic bowl with the remains of the squid stew. "Leslie," he says, giving my shoulder a squeeze, "I haven't even asked you about the art cooperatives you thought of establishing in the States when you went back the last time. How did it go?"

"What cooperatives?" I say, my mind blank for a moment before recapturing the memory. "Oh yes, the mountain crafts. No, it never got off the ground. I mean, I never got it together."

"That's too bad," Alexandra says. "It sounded like such a great idea."

"It seems easier to talk than to carry something out," I say, discouragement evident in my voice.

"Leslie is a great assistant with the literacy work we're doing in Madrugada," Helena says as she stacks the dirty dishes on her side of the table.

"But, Leslie, don't you think the U.S. is the best place for Americans with a political consciousness to be working?" Tiago rests comfortably back against his chair, arms folded across his chest.

"It's something I've been thinking about," I say.

Joana gives me a quizzical look and I quickly stand up to help Alexandra clear the table.

On the ride home in the car the air feels heavy with a quiet tension between Miguel, Helena, and me. Joana talks about the weather, the kids, the night, the dinner. She doesn't seem to mind that no one talks with her.

As the car pulls up to the curb outside of Helena's apartment Helena leans over the front seat to say thank you and good night to Miguel and Joana. She opens the door and starts to step out, then turns back towards me, her eyes filled with questions. She raises her shoulders slightly and gives a small smile. "Good night," she says.

* * * * *

The next morning I tap on the bright red door.

"Bom dia, Leslie. Come in."

Helena is dressed in a white painter's smock and baggy green pants, each leg wrapped at the ankle with bright multicolored silk scarves.

She closes the door behind us. We embrace and hold each other close for a moment.

She steps back. "Would you like some tea?"

"I just had coffee," I say.

Helena stops and for a moment rocks indecisively back and forth on the heels of her shoes. "Well, let me close up my paint and clean the brushes."

She walks to the standing rack where several jars are opened. Keeping her back to me, she carefully screws on each lid. I stand quietly in the middle of the room and watch. She takes a fat round brush with red paint and a medium size one with blue and drops them into a jar of murky blue-black water. She picks up the jar and, still not meeting my eyes, walks past me into the kitchen where she dumps the water and brushes into the sink. She turns on the tap and lets it run full force. I stand in the kitchen doorway and watch her clean the brushes, her hands immersed in the swirling red and blue paint that rushes from the bristles.

"How are you doing?" I ask, breaking the tight silence.

"I've gotten some painting done this morning." She looks at me for a moment and then turns her attention again to the brushes and the running water.

I stand still in the silence, waiting for Helena to show the way past this chosen distance. When she called this morning her voice wavered between indifference and sadness. This was such a contrast to her normal enthusiasm I was caught off guard, unsure how to respond.

Helena finishes with the cleaning, shakes the excess water from the brushes. She lays them on the side of the sink, wipes her hands on a towel, and turns towards me.

"We need to talk," she says, finally meeting my eyes.

We both take a seat at the small round table.

"I need some tea," Helena says. Scooting out of the seat, she grabs the teapot and fills it with water.

When Helena joins me again, I reach across the small table and take her hand in mine. Her skin is warm from the tea mug. Her eyes are bloodshot.

"How did you sleep last night?" I ask.

"Not very well. I did a lot of thinking."

I hold her fingers and run my thumb over the

152

back of her hand. I brace myself, thinking of all the ways she could end our relationship. We sit quietly, the smell of hot tea and chocolate cookies stirring the air.

"Leslie," she begins.

I bite a cookie and taste a rush of chocolate.

"I don't know if I can do this," she continues.

This really is it. Next she'll explain why she can't be my lover.

Helena takes her hand away from mine and holds it over the warm tea. "I've been thinking about the challenges you've brought into my life."

"Helena," I interject, anxious about what she's going to say. "If you don't want to see me anymore you can just say so."

"Leslie, that's not what I'm talking about."

"No?"

"It's not so much about us, but about my life in Portugal." She looks out the kitchen window. I too look at the view of the neighboring backside veranda where a line of shirts and skirts, white underpants and dark slacks flutter back and forth.

"Now I know what it feels like," Helena says. "I know how the villagers feel when I ask them to take responsibility for their lives." She turns her concentration to the mug of tea cupped between her hands. "I ask these people to put their fears aside, to face injustice and to challenge systems that work against them, but I don't have the courage to do it myself. I can't do it, Leslie. I don't want to be open here."

"I understand, Helena." I wrap my fingers around her wrist and hold it gently. "I'm sorry your involvement with me has made it difficult for you."

"Don't apologize for that." She leans across the table and places her cheek next to mine. "Don't apologize for making me think. I just don't know if I'm strong enough to continue living here with my eyes open. I might have to leave . . ." She leans back and looks into my eyes.

"Like me and the States," I say. "I need time away to get perspective."

"Maybe I'll go to England for a longer stay, maybe six months or a year. There's a community of support there."

"It's difficult when you feel so alone," I say. I scoot my chair around to her side of the table and nestle my face into the curve of her neck to try to hold back the tears filling my eyes. I breathe slow into the warm smell of her body.

"That's why I want to go to England. I don't want to close off this part of myself, to hide in the closet, as you say." Helena strokes my hair. I kiss her lips, feeling her cheeks wet with tears. "How will you feel if I leave?" she asks.

We lean our foreheads together, both of us crying freely now. "It's so hard," I say, "but I understand because I ask myself the same question about staying."

She pulls her head back, shifts in her seat, touches my wet face. "You could come to England," she says.

"I would love to be with you, Helena, I would. But if I leave Portugal I'll most likely go back to the States. We both know that's where I need to be working as an American. I'm still not certain what I want to do."

"Someday people will be more open here," Helena

says. "Maybe after a stay in England I'll even return to Portugal and help make those changes."

"Helena, your determination makes me question my own choices. Am I only running away by living in Portugal?"

"Allow yourself some time," Helena says. She wipes her eyes and sighs deeply. "How is it at the house with Miguel and the others?"

"Cristina and I are still avoiding each other," I say, "and I haven't seen Miguel since last night. He went to Lisbon this morning on hospital business and won't be back for a few days. It's good for us to have a break right now."

"I'm so angry with him," Helena says. "He knew what he was doing in trying to set me up, didn't he?"

"I think so."

"What about Isabel?"

"She's fine," I say, "and Joana seems rather oblivious to everything."

"That doesn't sound like Joana."

"Maybe it's her way of dealing," I suggest. "Have you really decided about England?"

"I think so."

"When will you go?"

"I'd already planned to visit for a week just after the art show opening. While I'm there I can talk with my friends about arranging a longer stay after the spring semester."

We curl up on the lumpy old couch António put in the studio the day before. The sun, streaming through the window above our heads, warms the room and we lie in lazy comfort.

When Helena leaves for her afternoon class I walk

155

to the café down the street and call Joana at home and make plans to meet her there in an hour. I take a long walk through the streets, thinking about this shifting landscape.

I hadn't considered the possibility of Helena leaving. It was always a picture of me packing my bags. I feel a small space in my heart begin to ache and wish we hadn't gotten involved. But at the same time I remember the pleasures of the past weeks and have no regrets. If she moves it's not a personal rejection of me, but a positive choice for herself. Maybe that's true of many choices, even Deirdre's moving away.

In the distance I can hear the fruit man calling out, "Apples, oranges," his melodious voice familiar music in the afternoon air.

* * * * *

When I arrive at the house Joana comes sweeping into the living room with an exaggerated swing in her body. "Are you planning something I don't know about?" She stops in front of me, her hip jutted out, her hand extending several envelopes towards me. "You received five letters from the States today. Could they possibly be job offers?"

"Why do you say that?"

"Because I always think you're going to leave."

"Come and sit with me." I pat the couch.

She drops the letters on my lap. I flip through them. "From Sarah, my mom, one of my sisters, and one from an old job. I hope they forgot to pay me some money and this is an unexpected check. And, hey, a letter from Audrey."

"What does she write?" Joana asks.

"Let's talk first, then we can go through this assortment of American gossip."

Joana joins me on the couch, kicking off her shoes and stretching out her legs.

"We haven't had a chance for a real talk the past few days," I say.

"I guess I'm more preoccupied the closer we get to the exhibit."

"It'll be a great success," I say.

"I hope so. I'm already trying to figure out what we can follow this with. I don't want to lose the momentum."

"You're great, Joana."

"Why is that?"

"Because you offer the spirit behind this show."

"Oh, everyone's involved. It's a cooperative effort."

"But you're the one who's maintained the vision throughout the whole process. I remember the look on Raul and Miguel's faces when they tried to start from a practical place and you were there talking about freedom. Without that the exhibit would be just like any other show."

"Maybe so," Joana says.

"Joana, how do you feel about me still being in the house?" I ask.

"What do you mean?"

"Are you getting tired of me?"

"Of course not. As far as I'm concerned you can stay as long as you want."

"I think I'm starting to cramp people's space. Cristina seems awfully moody and Miguel keeps pulling further away.

"Miguel is overworked and Cristina is always like that with her period," Joana protests.

"Her period can't be going on for weeks."

"It's probably her boyfriend. She thinks you have to be depressed at least half of the time or it's not really love."

"Joana, she's bothered by my being here."

"What makes you say that?" Joana asks.

"Because she never looks at me and she doesn't talk to me anymore."

"Leslie, she's eighteen years old, half the time she doesn't talk to me either. Don't worry about it."

"Look we can't ignore the fact that this situation is becoming uncomfortable. It would be better if I just moved out."

"I don't want you to move. I'll talk with Cristina and Miguel. They've got to stop if they're being rude to you. I won't have my closest friend run out of my own house."

The phone rings and Constança summons Joana.

As soon as they leave the room I rip open Audrey's letter. As I expected, she tells me about the projects she's involved with, and all the interesting people she works with, and if I consider returning to the States I should pick Albuquerque because it's such a beautiful place and there's so much going on. She writes about the work with Central Americans and makes comparisons to the literacy work in Portugal. People have been killed in Guatemala and El Salvador for simple things we take for granted, like giving health care or teaching literacy. Large numbers of European refugees have been accepted into the U.S. in contrast to the hundreds of Latin

Americans that are deported back to certain death. I read through her letter, trying not to respond to the appeal that has already entered my heart. I know what I want to do because I have been thinking about it since Audrey first told me the stories. This feels right, but I don't yet want to face it.

* * * * *

I invite Isabel for afternoon tea. We take the steetcar down to one of the cafés in town where she orders several pastries and café com leite.

"Constança is always telling me to watch my weight," Isabel says. "I hate when she does that, so I like to eat as much as possible when she's not around." She gives me a rebellious grin when the waiter comes with a plate of croissants and chocolate éclairs.

"So, Leslie, do you and I have something important to talk about?"

"How did you guess?" I say.

"Because you look so serious and nervous." She takes a large bite from an éclair and then licks the chocolate from her lips.

"Sometimes you're too perceptive," I say.

"Oh, you can never be too clear."

I want to say something about truth out of the mouth of babes. But I remember what Audrey said about not being an ageist so I keep my mouth shut and try to keep open to wise things from wherever they come.

"You're a pretty open person," I say. "How do you think you got that way?"

"I guess from my parents."

I imagine this litany passed on from mother to daughter.

"Well, I want to ask you what's up with Cristina. Is she having a problem with me or am I reading it all wrong?"

"She's not too happy about you and Helena," Isabel explains in her easy manner.

"You say that so casually."

"I know what people think — that it's not normal. But, hey, love is about as normal as you can get. What difference does it make who you love?"

"You're amazing, Isabel."

"Why is that?"

"Because you're so unaffected by society's norms."

"Oh, I have to work at it. You know, I have this friend in school who's fallen in love with this guy from the marketplace. They're from entirely different worlds. It'll probably never work out because when her parents find out they'll just absolutely forbid it. And, I have to admit, at first I didn't like that she was going with him."

"Why not?"

"I never met anyone like him. You know, fourth grade education and growing and selling vegetables his whole life. I just thought those people were really different than us."

"What do you think now?"

"That of course there's differences because of how we're raised, but what the two of them do shouldn't be anybody's business. Maybe they could really be happy together, but not if they have to keep sneaking around."

"Like me and Helena," I say.

160

"Hey, that's right," Isabel says with a surprised look of recognition.

"What do you think I should do about Cristina?" I ask.

"I don't know," Isabel says.

14

Rhythmic sounds of a wooden loom can be heard as Helena and I approach a house with door and windows open to the afternoon air. Walking the length of the village of Madrugada we have passed similar rooms, where the rhythmic thumping of wood was accompanied here and there with a solitary voice singing lonesome sweet tunes.

"Bom dia, Senhora Maria de Conceição."

"Bom dia, meninas." Senhora Maria flags us into the room with her firm, muscular arm. She's wearing a sleeveless blouse, a skirt, and rubber fisherman's boots. Thick, dark, shoulder length hair is held back from her ruddy face with a black scarf. While Helena and the woman talk I stand quietly, looking over the colorful material stretched out in the loom.

"This is a bedspread," Helena explains, trying to pull me into the conversation.

I smile at Senhora Maria. "It's very beautiful."

Senhora Maria explains in great detail how methodically the strings are laid out. I look at the hundreds of pieces of thread and can't imagine the time this takes. "It must require great patience," I say.

"We learn this work as children and we learn patience from our life in the village. We don't live like you girls in the city where your life is hectic and rushed. There you have much to distract you, but here what we have is time and the work that is necessary."

Helena explains about the art exhibit and how she wants to include some of the work from the weaving cooperative. Dona Maria thinks it's a good idea. She leads us on a search through the various houses on the one road that runs the length of the village. Several pieces are chosen and eagerly handed over, the names of the women written on tape attached to the backs.

"I want all of you to come to the show," Helena says to Dona Maria.

"If Helena says it will be good for us then we will come."

"It will give exposure for the cooperative," Helena explains.

"And it will show that necessary work is also art," I say.

163

We go upstairs, where Senhora Maria offers us wine, bread, and slices of home-cured sausage. She shows us her sleeping baby and explains that her other children are at school and her husband is in the fields. She opens a big trunk and pulls out a colorfully embroidered cloth used for keeping bread warm. "Menina," she says, extending the cloth to me. "You take this to your country when you go. You show them what we make here."

Later at Joana and Miguel's I sit quietly through dinner, listening to Zé and Isabel talk about school. Joana prods them with questions about their assignments and the upcoming new term. Cristina's at an evening class, so I don't have to face her icy silence. Since Miguel's return from Lisbon he seems to be keeping a diplomatic distance, working late at the hospital, choosing easy conversation over dinner, and retiring to bed early. A part of me wants to maintain this false tranquility until I move out and put some space between us, but I know I need to talk about Cristina. I wait for the right time, but it never seems to come. I let another night go by, feeling the tension build out of proportion inside of me. I promise myself I'll talk with Joana and Miguel.

* * * * *

I stand quietly in the doorway and look at Joana sitting on the couch working with a ball of yarn. Miguel is gazing out the sliding glass doors onto the veranda. It's so peaceful and I don't want to disturb the quiet, but I promised myself last night. I step into the room.

164

"Joana and Miguel, we need to talk." The words run fast out of my mouth.

"Sure. What's up?" Joana says, looking up from her ball of yarn.

"Well, can we go for a ride or something? I'm kind of nervous about this."

"Don't say you're leaving the country," Joana says. "I don't want to hear it."

"No, it's not that, Joana."

"Why not be American and be direct with it," Miguel says, his impatient tone throwing me off balance. I step backwards as he moves into the center of the room.

"I don't want to be American with this. I want to do it Portuguese style."

"Is it about Cristina?" he asks.

The surprise is immediate, and must be unmistakable on my face. "I don't want to talk about it here." I'm rapidly losing direction about how to proceed.

"Cristina's already spoken with me," Miguel shoots back.

"Miguel!" Joana snaps as she jumps to her feet.

"Cristina's upset about Helena and Leslie. It does need to be talked about."

"God," I say in English.

"What has Cristina told you?" Joana asks.

Miguel and I both start to talk at once.

"Go ahead, Miguel," I say. "I want to hear what Cristina said to you."

"She thinks it's sick what you're doing."

"Miguel, what did you say to her?" Joana looks back and forth between the two of us.

165

"Joana, she's a kid. She's confused. What could I say?"

"That there's nothing wrong with what Leslie and Helena are doing!"

"I don't know if I agree with that." Miguel turns his head sharply towards Joana, the tension in the room sparking like heat lightning.

"I thought you were open-minded," I say.

"Some things don't fit into our culture," Miguel replies disdainfully.

"Who decides that, Miguel?" I retort.

"There are some things you can't understand."

"I understand that you're trying to shut off an entire segment of the population!"

"In America it's different," he says.

"You want people to live hidden lives!"

"I'm not sure it's normal." Miguel speaks in a loud sarcastic voice as he thrusts his head forward in the space between us.

"I don't really care what you think," I shout, staring defiantly at Miguel.

"Wait a minute!" Joana says, stepping between us.

"What Helena and I do has nothing to do with you, Miguel! Or is that what bothers you?"

"Wait a minute!" Joana says, placing a hand on each of our arms. "Let's talk about this."

"We are talking," Miguel says.

"I can't believe you feel this way," Joana says to Miguel, surprise evident in her voice.

"Listen," Miguel says, "I don't like having to deal with this any more than either of you do."

"I don't have a choice about it," I say. "This is

my life. Anyway, I have an easy solution. It's time for me to move out."

"I don't want you to move because of this, Joana says.

"No. Susana and António have asked me and you know I've been planning to move."

"But not like this," she implores.

"I think it's just as well for now," Miguel interjects.

"Miguel, I can't believe you're talking this way!" Joana replies angrily. "I have never heard such prejudice from you!"

"Listen, I'm not saying what Leslie chooses is wrong." He looks at me scornfully. "But how can you have criticism about American influence when you're doing exactly the same thing?"

"What in the world are you talking about?" I say.

"Helena's been brought over by your American influence. She wasn't involved like this before you came. Someone needs to protect her —"

"Don't show your ignorance," I say, rising from the seat and heading for the stairs.

I frantically throw clothes and books into my suitcase, my mind racing to figure out a plan. When there's a light knock at the door I want to scream.

Joana's voice comes softly and sympathetically from the other side of the door. "Leslie, let me come in, okay?"

I open the door and stand defiantly in the entrance.

"Leslie, I'm really sorry," she says.

"It comes with the territory," I say sarcastically.

She looks past me at the open suitcase crammed

with wadded clothes and I see tears in her eyes. I loosen my stance and step away from the door. She follows me into the room and goes to my suitcase where she starts pulling out clothes to refold them neatly.

"Can I call Helena for you?" she asks.

"No," I say, trying to soften my voice from the rage I feel. "I'm going to Susana and António's."

"Do you have enough money?" she says.

"Don't worry about it."

"I do worry," she says, breaking into tears. We hold each other and cry.

* * * * *

When Susana opens the door she looks surprised at my overly heavy suitcase and backpack. "That's what I call a quick decision," she says. "Come in. I've had your bed made for a week."

When I start to tell her the story Susana takes my hand and leads me into the bathroom where she fills the tub with steaming water. "Climb in," she says.

I pull off my clothes without even thinking about her being there. I climb into the large swayback tub, sink into the water up to my chin, and pull the washcloth hot and dripping over my face.

"Poor baby," she says. "Do you want me to call Helena for you?"

"No."

"Well, let me get you something cold to drink and I'll roll a joint if you like."

I take the cold glass of Coca-Cola, but decline the joint. Susana sits on the floor by the tub and fills the room with the sweet smell of marijuana. We talk about everything, except what just happened. Later, amid the fresh smell of clean sheets I feel comfortable and cared for, as though Susana and I have been long-time friends.

* * * * *

For days I stay alone in the room, sleeping late, reading books, coming out for long baths. Susana cancels my English lessons for the week. She and António make hot soup and mostly leave me alone for the first three days.

On day four Helena storms into the apartment, saying, defiantly, "Maybe I am being pushy but I'm tired of your American need for space. Why are you letting this fight with Miguel get in the way of our friendship? I have a right to say something about it because it's affecting me too!"

She's an inch from my face. I want to push back and put more space between us. But I stand unmoving, trying to keep my eyes and heart open, struggling against an urge to run.

"I'm sorry." My voice strains against the tears that well up in my eyes.

Helena reaches out and enfolds me in her arms. "You don't have to be sorry," she whispers into my ear. I push my face against her shirt, the smell of her body a familiar comfort.

"I've missed you," she says.

"I don't want to drag you into this mess," I say, looking into her dark eyes.

"Don't worry about it. I'm already in it. I can take care of myself."

"Why the change of attitude?"

"I'm tired of being afraid."

"Then it's not bad this is all stirred up? That's why I didn't call you. I thought you'd be mad at me."

"I've decided I'm definitely going to live in England, at least for some months, and that decision has freed me up a lot. This hasn't been an easy time, but knowing you has helped me really look at my life."

"What if you can't come home again?" I say.

"I'll take the chance."

"I feel responsible for what's happening to you."

Helena takes my shoulders in both hands. "Leslie, I know how you feel. When the villagers get in the middle of a heated struggle with the government because of something I've suggested, I want to tell them to give up and retreat back to their predictable lives. I'm afraid the whole thing is going to blow up and make a mess of things. But I try not to let those fears control me because the only way anything is going to change is to be open."

"You said you can't be open here."

"That's why I want to go to England. Hopefully I'll develop strength and inner resources so I can return here in the future and help with some changes."

"Like me and the States," I say. "I lost my sense of direction there. Knowing you, watching you work — I've rediscovered a focus."

"I'm glad," Helena says.

"Then you don't regret knowing me?"

"Of course not. The tragedy would be to live my life blindly."

170

She kisses my cheek and tousles my hair. We make our way to the bedroom where we lie on the bed and hold each other. An hour later, when António and Susana arrive home, Helena and I are sitting comfortably in the living room drinking tea.

The four of us go to a small restaurant outside of town where food is brought in large steaming platters to the table.

"Joana's called several times," António says.

"I don't know what to say to her," I reply.

"You can't leave this hanging indefinitely between the two of you," Helena says.

After dinner we take a long drive in the country. Helena and I sit in the back seat holding each other silently through the drive until António speaks.

"It's a lousy mess," he says.

"Why are straight people like this?" I ask.

"You're asking me?" he says. "I'm not exactly your typical heterosexual."

"I didn't think Miguel was either."

"Give the guy some time," António says. "He's got this macho image to work through. He'll come around."

"I don't know if I'm ready to wait for that."

* * * * *

Several days later António loans me his car and I drive into the countryside, bundled in a sweater and a light winter jacket against the cooling weather. I pull the car over on a deserted road and walk out into a rolling field. I walk for a long time, with firm and consistent strides. The brisk pace and the sun on

171

my back warm me. I walk until my legs are tired and the sun moves across a certain stretch of sky.

I haven't seen Joana, Miguel, or the kids in over a week. It feels completely strange. What's the point of being in Portugal if I can't see the people who mean so much to me? I continue walking until my legs tire and my restless mind settles down. I turn back, knowing I can't run away from this. It's too important to me. When I get back to the apartment I call Joana and we make plans to meet in town.

We choose a table by the window and Joana places our order for two coffees with milk. We ease back into our connection by talking about the art exhibit which is opening this weekend.

"You've got to say you'll come," she says. "You know how much this means to me."

"Of course I'm coming."

"Good." She reaches across the table to squeeze my hand. "I've missed you. I keep thinking you're going to leave. I've had this repeated dream that you already left for America. You're going back there, aren't you?"

"I'm not sure, Joana."

"What have you been doing this past week?"

"A lot of thinking."

"I figured that. I hope you don't leave because of Miguel's stupidity."

"Joana, what Miguel's doing goes on everywhere. I can tell you similar or worse experiences friends of mine have had back in the States."

"I'm sorry," she says. "I'm really sorry."

"If I do go back it won't be because of Miguel and Cristina's attitudes. For a long time I've been trying to figure out the best place for me to be. I want to be happy and I want to be working in a way that means something. Since I received that letter from Audrey —"

"I knew that was it," Joana says.

"Well, I think Tiago is right. Maybe the best place for an American to be working right now is in the States."

"Just because you were born there doesn't mean you owe loyalty to a piece of geography."

"It's more than geography, Joana. What I'm talking about is my struggle with that culture. I come from there and because of that I have responsibility. I can't close my eyes and run away. If I want things to change then I need to be a part of it."

"I hate that wide ocean sometimes," Joana says. "It keeps you away from me."

"It makes me sad too. Joana . . . there's something else you need to know. It's hard for me to live here because I have to be so closed about my relationship with Helena."

"It's new for us, Leslie. We aren't very good at handling it."

"Why is it so difficult?"

"Miguel feels protective of Helena."

"What's he protecting her from? Me? Joana, he really hurt me the other day."

Tears glisten the edges of Joana's eyes. She starts to speak, but falters and places her hand over her mouth. She looks across the table at me, her deep brown eyes filled with sadness.

"Maybe I shouldn't have told you about my life," I say.

She wraps her hands around the coffee cup, shaking her head. "No, Leslie, silence would not work between us."

"Joana, you need to help educate other people."

"How?" she asks incredulously. "I'm so ignorant."

"But you're open," I say. "That's the first step."

15

On the hard plank benches in the church of Madrugada three women, Helena, and I talk about the weaving cooperative. This is the finance committee. We discuss at great length figures on sales, quantity and the development of new markets. I try to keep my focus, but am quickly bored and drift off to my own thoughts.

A few minutes later Helena pulls me back with a question, "What can you say about that, Leslie?"

I give her a quizzical look, but she doesn't rescue me. So I have to say, "Sorry. I missed the point."

Helena goes on to explain, "Maria de Conceição says the women wonder why when the weavings hang in the art exhibit we charge so much more than when someone buys them for regular use?"

"It's people's perceptions," I say, thinking how often we define our own experience through other people's opinions.

* * * * *

I decide to spend the two-day Christmas holiday at the shore on my own. I pitch my tent on a stretch of isolated beach and sit inside the familiar, contained walls, looking out towards that wide expanse of horizon. The air is cold off the water, but the sun is warm against the yellow nylon sides.

For an hour I watch the waves come to shore, the gulls soaring on invisible currents between land and sea. The crashing water and the cry of the birds are a beacon to this wide open space inside my chest.

There is no easy answer plays through my brain like a refrain from an unsung song. The waves rush against the shore, a background rhythm.

"What is calling me?" I say aloud.

I imagine the enormous space between this shoreline and the other called home. I'll never be able to integrate them because always there will be this separation of the wide, deep blue ocean.

"What's the point?" I wonder. Silence is the easy choice. I remember the village women who rise before dawn to study. They understand that reading and writing aren't simply skills, but a way to think for themselves. I know I can't turn away from what's calling me. But what is the answer?

176

If I think hard enough I'll figure this out, but my brain is trying too hard. Finally I stretch out on my sleeping bag and fall into a heavy sleep.

When I awake the sun has moved into dusk. The lines between sky and ocean are hazy, almost invisible. I pull myself out of the tent and follow the sand along the shoreline. Low tide further exposes the beach, changing the terrain. Several fish left by the receding waters lie in the sand. Here one is missing a head, there a fat, red organ lays half way out of the belly of another. If I were eating this fish on a plate I wouldn't think twice, but to see it open and raw like this feels ugly. Why is it so hard to accept what is natural?

Past the dead fish I find a clear spot of sand where I squat and watch night move across the land and overtake the ocean. It's a deep darkness with no lights around. I breathe full and easy, calming a slight fear that plays along my edges.

"It's okay here," I say. "It's okay."

I hear the tide begin to shift as the waves move more fully into shore. Every day this beach widens, recedes, and then widens again, a witness to both constancy and change. I wrap my arms close about my chest and feel the rhythmic beat of my own heart. My body's the only home I can really claim.

I stand and retrace my path, the sound of the water as my guide. This is what it must feel like to be blind, trusting your body totally to the elements.

After walking a distance I realize I can follow the water, but I can't find my tent. I wish I'd brought my flashlight. I imagine myself spending the night searching with hands outstretched into the dark for my small, yellow gypsy home.

Have I walked only a few hundred yards or several miles? Time seems unmarkable with no landscape against which to measure it. "Okay, don't panic," I say, as I feel panic rising inside my chest. "Have a group meeting with yourself." I squat again on the shore, wondering if a dead fish is under me or near me. Remember, I tell myself, all those anti-nuclear demos where we sat in circles to discuss the next possible action. I smile and slowly match my breathing to the rhythm of the waves.

It's strange how panic can rise against the unknown; how distortion is a quick response. What's the worst that can happen? That I won't sleep tonight because I'm not comfortable enough to curl up in the sand, afraid of sand crabs crawling onto my body. Do they even have those tiny little creatures here that make me scream and scurry off in fear? What a silly response, fear against that which is most natural.

I remember the tarot reading Sarah gave for my departure. Allow compassion not only for others, she said, but also for yourself. It's okay to be afraid. Everyone is. It's what you do afterwards that makes a difference. Silence falls away from me as a lone sea gull suddenly calls out into the night.

Home is where the heart is echoes in my head, a trite saying embroidered on my Aunt Jenny's kitchen towels. Aunt Jenny's kitchen, where chocolate chip cookies and a tall glass of iced milk were sure answers to every tribulation. She never quoted from the Bible to me, like Grandma did. She'd just take out the cookie sheet, grease it with shortening, crack eggs into a big bowl, and begin the mixing of a fresh batch, filling the kitchen with the warm, sweet smell.

It was there I learned the thrill of talking, Aunt Jenny and I serving audience to each other in turn.

It was she who encouraged my travels, her wanderlust in direct contrast to her circumstance. She had always lived with my grandmother, staying on at the age of twenty when Grandpa died, and for forty years afterwards because Grandma lived into her eighties. Aunt Jenny at age sixty was finally free, but she said she was too old for changes, resigning herself to that big old house of her childhood.

Eventually she rented out rooms to college students, needing the extra cash for expenses. The living room now serves as a women's center and the kitchen phone is a crisis hot line. Aunt Jenny, living in the midst of youthful students, now wears that shocked, happy smile that change can bring. There are many ways to travel, many ways to make home.

Off to my left the moon crests above the horizon, the tip of a big orange ball. Slowly it reveals its fullness into the sky, lighting a path back to the tent and the warm cuddle of my sleeping bag.

The ocean rocks me to sleep. The moon calls forth the rhythmic tune.

* * * * *

It's the day before the opening. Helena and I are the first to arrive at the gallery. When Joana enters she gives Helena a kiss and then wraps her arms around me and pulls me against her. We hold each other tight. "I miss you at the house," she whispers.

"I miss you too." We give each other a kiss and then let go.

Helena, Joana, and I quickly scan the stacks of

179

paintings leaning against the walls and several pieces of sculpture standing in one corner.

"I can't believe we waited until the last day to do this," Joana says, a bit frantic.

"Do you think we can pull it off?" Helena says. "I mean, look at all of this."

"Of course we will," Joana responds, her voice now more sure.

Raul and Alexandra arrive and we all begin work, grouping the paintings and then regrouping them twice more. We take turns holding them up against the wall, trying different combinations. Raul and Alexandra add to the complication by picking up various pieces of sculpture and moving them about the room. After an hour and a half not one frame has been hung. I start to laugh and we all end up bent over ourselves, laughter echoing off the high ceilings.

Alexandra brings out a bottle of wine and we sit in the middle of one of the rooms. After emptying the bottle with a few passes around the circle, we stretch out on the high polished wood floors and look eye level at the sketches, paintings, and photographs placed around the baseboards.

"Let's just leave them where they are," Joana says.

"It would give the babies a good perspective," Raul adds.

Two hours later everything is in place and properly identified. Joana, Helena, and I decide to take ourselves out to dinner for celebration.

We go to a small restaurant where the tables are made of long wooden planks rubbed smooth and shiny from years of use. We choose one table where two or three small groups are already seated. Elbow to elbow we enter into the atmosphere of loud talk and cheer.

We drink big mugs of wine, and cut thick slices of broa. The bowls of soup are a meal in themselves with large pieces of carrots and potatoes, beans and slices of cabbage. This is followed by a platter of fish, boiled potatoes and rice. And that is followed by a huge serving of pork, rice, and chunks of potatoes cooked in pork sauce. Every time my mug is emptied it's filled again with the sweet red wine. We eat and talk for hours.

At ten o'clock dessert is served. I know I'm not going to be able to walk out of this place. I eat leite cream and bread pudding, and have a taste of Joana's chocolate mousse. Finally, we decline the fruit and cheese, and chase our satisfaction out into the night.

"I think we better take a walk," Helena says.

The three of us link arms and take over the middle of the street. Our impromptu singing greets the night air with a happy tune, and I feel at home with myself.

* * * * *

The next day Helena and I talk excitedly about tonight's exhibit opening. Helena's eyes are lit torches in her enthusiasm. I'm very close to her excitement, but still only an observer. This is Helena's passion, ready to be revealed to a wider audience.

"I don't want to stop doing this," she says. "I want a new opening every week!"

"Maybe the next step is for you to open a gallery."

"Can you imagine?" she says with a look of

delight. "Unfortunately I don't have the financial base for it."

"Maybe the man from Germany who offered money for this show will want to fund something else," I suggest.

"This town is too small to host another gallery and anyway I'll be leaving soon."

"Maybe you'll get involved with galleries in England," I say.

"Someday I'd like to go to New York. That place must be so big you can do anything."

I reach across the table and run my hand through Helena's auburn curls. She bends her head into the flow of my touch and smiles across the space between us. "I wish we both could go there now," I say.

"It would be wonderful to have you help me weather the cultural shock." She leans forward and places a kiss on my shoulder. "But for the moment our paths seem to be leading off in different directions."

I think about the pleasure of our relationship where forever has never been a pressing concern, knowing that the right things will happen at the right time. This is natural motion, like waves moving to shore. I look across the space between us and think about Joana with whom forever has seemed unquestionable. I know there is an endless and boundless motion here; love as both constancy and change.

* * * * *

Helena and I arrive fashionably late for the opening, her nervous energy having held her back

182

from an immediate desire to plunge in. She said she wanted to wait until the place was crowded — exactly how she wanted to experience it. On the way over we both wondered nervously, What if no one's there?

As soon as we open the door I feel a rush of excitement at seeing the crowd. Helena squeezes my hand and pushes off into the room. I continue standing inside the doorway, viewing the first wide room.

Zé comes bounding out of the crowd. "Isabel and I've been waiting for you to come." He gives me a shy kiss on the cheek. "Guess what? Everybody loves her painting."

"Let me tell it," Isabel says as she lands beside us, wrapping her arms around me for a big hug. "Leslie," she says, "everybody loves my painting!"

"Fantastic!" I say, patting her on the shoulder.

"Where have you been?" Isabel says. "I've been dying for you to get here! I miss you so much! I want you to meet these friends of mine, and I want you to try these great chocolates that Raul brought. António and Susana are here too," she continues.

"Where shall we start?" I ask.

"With the chocolates, of course."

As Isabel sips on a small glass of wine, I allow an overly delicious chocolate to melt in my mouth, trying not to chew it. Around the room I see a variety of people: the very formal art critic types next to bohemians and punks, village women with their children clinging close to them and outside, visible through the windows, their men standing in a small cluster on the sidewalk with wine and cigarettes to pass the evening.

"Where's the rest of your family?" I ask the kids.

"Oh, around," Isabel says, as I watch Joana and Helena wander by in the next room.

I leave the kids with the chocolates and begin to slowly view the paintings and drawings we so carefully hung the day before. I'm glad I got to see them first without such a crowd. Now each of the works takes on a new dimension as I listen to people around me comment and jostle for a better view.

Teresa and Paulo greet me in front of several large abstracts. My earlier concern about what they heard regarding my moving out seems irrelevant against their excited energy, as vibrant as the background of colorful paintings.

Teresa's stomach is huge and she leans uncomfortably into her lower back, her hands holding the sides of her stomach.

"Aren't you due soon?" I ask.

"Not soon enough," she says with a smile.

António joins us. He's wearing the funky tie-dyed shirt I had Sarah send from Woodstock and his hair now nearly reaches his shoulders. Teresa smiles uncomfortably and Paulo sports an obvious sneer. António's oblivious to both of them. With the fanfare of a drag queen he pulls me away to find Susana.

"I want to see the paintings," I say.

"You have all night," he replies.

We find Susana and start from where she is, looking again at the work. António stands to my right and talks nonstop about his impressions of each painting.

Again I see Joana in the crowd. This time our eyes meet and she smiles at me. She's with someone I don't know and she returns with intense concentration to him.

184

As we move along the wall we come across Maria de Conceição and a small group of women from the village of Madrugada. They are standing protectively beside one of their weavings. António and Susana wander away and I enter into the talk of this small circle of women.

"How are you doing this evening?" I ask.

"This is a new experience for us," the taller woman says.

"Have you heard comments about your work?"

"Yes, people seem to like it," Maria de Conceição says.

"Tell her about that man," someone says from behind me.

"What man?" I ask.

"Oh, it's nothing," Maria says. "It was only a silly mistake, a silly joke for us to laugh about."

A young woman I haven't met says, "Maria went to get us some drinks and when she was walking back this man said he would like a drink too."

"You mean he was asking her to join him?" I ask.

"No," they all say at once.

"He thought she was the maid," the young woman explains.

I start to get mad, but they just laugh. "You see, we know we really aren't a part of this crowd."

"But you are," I say. "People want to see your work, they appreciate it."

"But we're not a part of this crowd," the young woman says.

"I'm happy you're here and so is Helena," I say, just as Helena walks by. I wrap my arm around her waist and pull her into our small circle.

185

We watch Isabel wander by with the friends she'd told me about. One is a girl obviously from the city and the other a village boy, the two of them wrapped arm in arm.

"Who doesn't belong here?" I say. The women raise their shoulders in a questioning response.

Finally I pull myself away to view more of the work. I stand in front of Miguel's drawing of our faces and wonder why I haven't seen him here. I look at the depiction he's made of each of our friends. The details are very exact. These are the people who have such a special place in my heart yet two of them now won't talk to me. I'm surprised at my own calm acceptance of their silence. I no longer feel the need to defend myself. They've made their choices. Looking at the circle of friends drawn in black ink, I know we are all a part of the same world, whether we accept everyone or not.

As I turn away from the drawing I see Miguel against the far wall watching me. He quickly turns and heads in the opposite direction. I then see Cristina see me and watch her eyes glaze over as she walks briskly past, two of her girlfriends in tow.

Damn this stupidity.

I return my concentration to the artwork and come across a most wonderful surprise. One of Joana's paintings has been switched. In place of the frantic birds in flight she's hung a drawing from her private sketch pad — two nude women in a serene pose, one standing behind the other, their gaze clear and direct towards the viewer. The two are separate; yet, with the hand of the woman behind touching lightly on the shoulder of the other, I sense in them a deep connection. At the bottom of the page, in a thin black line of Joana's handwriting, is the title, *In Honor of Friendship*. Tears jump into my eyes and my heart rushes with a pleasure that knows no hesitancy.

I look around and see Joana in a small group of people at the far end of the room. She looks in my direction and with a wave invites me to join them. She places a light kiss on my cheek and introduces me to the people with her. How very much I trust her love.

António and Susana join us and we decide to take a break into the refreshing chill of the night air. The village men are still in their little cluster, talking and taking deep draws on their cigarettes. We form another small group and talk about our impressions from the evening. Everyone appears quite pleased.

Joana says, "Leslie, let's walk down to the corner. We link arms and leave the jovial group behind.

"I was wondering," she says. "Has Miguel spoken with you this evening?"

"No he hasn't."

"He said he was going to. I've been making him think about his attitude."

"Thanks, Joana. But he hasn't made much of an effort."

"Maybe he still will."

"I saw the new drawing you put in the exhibit," I say. "It makes me proud to be your friend."

"You know it's for you, don't you?"

"Yes." Pleasure is a sure presence under my rib cage.

When we return to the gallery the rooms are less crowded. It's not easy for Miguel to avoid me. Finally he approaches.

"Leslie," he says. "Shall we talk?"

"Yes." I'm trying to keep my own vision clear and honorable.

He doesn't say anything and I wonder if he's waiting for me to start this conversation. I won't do it.

"Well," he says, watching his right foot play a toe-dance with the wood grain of the floor. "I guess I've been unfair. I mean, just closing you out." He hesitates and looks around the room as if expecting someone else to do this work for him.

I'm determined not to say anything. He has to be responsible.

"Well, I've been trying to figure this out," he continues, "and, I have to say honestly that I still have a reaction to your . . . your life, the way you choose to live it." Finally he looks up and meets my eyes, but only for a brief moment. He stares at the wall behind my head. There's a solid minute of silence between us that feels three hours long.

"And so," I finally say.

"I need time to work this through," he says.

"I won't wait for you," I say.

"Is this the end of our friendship?" He runs his hand through his hair and shifts from one foot to the other and back again.

"That depends, Miguel. If it's important to you you'll deal with yourself. And if not, well, yes, it's the end." I turn and head for any other place in the gallery.

In the next room I find Helena, Susana, and some other people in heated conversation. I join them without really listening to what they're talking about.

I think about Miguel and feel pride in how I handled myself.

Finally, after a few minutes, I settle down and tune into the hot debate around me. The group's talking about U.S. corporations and government involvements in Grenada, Guatemala, Nicaragua, El Salvador, South Africa, the Middle East. I've been standing here completely spaced out as these people talk with such passion about my country.

One of the women asks me angrily, "You are American, aren't you? What do you have to say?"

"I'm ashamed of my government."

"That isn't enough."

"I understand that," I answer, finally realizing that I'm the one who has to be responsible.

16

Helena and I awake early with dawn beginning to transform the dark night into a hazy gray-blue. We make love voraciously while the insistent sun approaches the horizon. When the first rays streak across the now light blue sky we hold our naked bodies close under the covers, knowing we can't elude this day of departure.

Helena gets up and lifts her suitcase onto the foot of the bed. I pull on a sweatshirt and go into the kitchen to make some tea. Too soon the taxi pulls up with a loud blare of its horn.

Maybe our choices aren't yet as clearly defined as we think."

I want to kiss Helena's lips, but there is a crowd of waiting passengers down the platform. We hear the whistle blow in the distance and watch the train come around the far bend. Helena drops her purse and wraps both of her arms around me.

As the train screeches to a halt behind us Helena places her lips on my cheek and we kiss. When the last person has cleared the platform the ticket taker leans out the door and beckons Helena with an outstretched arm. The shrill whistle blows and she climbs the couple of steps into the car.

We touch hands one last time as the train slowly begins to roll. She stands in the doorway waving until the train disappears around the long bend.

There is a sensation strong inside my chest, like when you lie stretched out on the ground so still for a very long time that at a certain point you're sure you feel the earth shift.

A few of the publications of
THE NAIAD PRESS, INC.
P.O. Box 10543 ● Tallahassee, Florida 32302
Phone (904) 539-5965
Mail orders welcome. Please include 15% postage.

FATAL REUNION by Claire McNab. 216 pp. 2nd Det. Inspec.
Carol Ashton mystery.   ISBN 0-941483-40-1 $8.95

KEEP TO ME STRANGER by Sarah Aldridge. 372 pp. Romance
set in a department store dynasty.   ISBN 0-941483-38-X   9.95

HEARTSCAPE by Sue Gambill. 204 pp. American lesbian in
Portugal.   ISBN 0-941483-33-9   8.95

IN THE BLOOD by Lauren Wright Douglas. 252 pp. Lesbian
science fiction adventure fantasy   ISBN 0-941483-22-3   8.95

THE BEE'S KISS by Shirley Verel. 216 pp. Delicate, delicious
romance.   ISBN 0-941483-36-3   8.95

RAGING MOTHER MOUNTAIN by Pat Emmerson. 264 pp.
Furosa Firechild's adventures in Wonderland. ISBN 0-941483-35-5 8.95

IN EVERY PORT by Karin Kallmaker. 228 pp. Jessica's sexy,
adventuresome travels.   ISBN 0-941483-37-7   8.95

OF LOVE AND GLORY by Evelyn Kennedy. 192 pp. Exciting
WWII romance.   ISBN 0-941483-32-0   8.95

CLICKING STONES by Nancy Tyler Glenn. 288 pp. Love
transcending time.   ISBN 0-941483-31-2   8.95

SURVIVING SISTERS by Gail Pass. 252 pp. Powerful love
story.   ISBN 0-941483-16-9   8.95

SOUTH OF THE LINE by Catherine Ennis. 216 pp. Civil War
adventure.   ISBN 0-941483-29-0   8.95

WOMAN PLUS WOMAN by Dolores Klaich. 300 pp. Supurb
Lesbian overview.   ISBN 0-941483-28-2   9.95

SLOW DANCING AT MISS POLLY'S by Sheila Ortiz Taylor.
96 pp. Lesbian Poetry   ISBN 0-941483-30-4   7.95

DOUBLE DAUGHTER by Vicki P. McConnell. 216 pp. A Nyla
Wade Mystery, third in the series.   ISBN 0-941483-26-6   8.95

HEAVY GILT by Delores Klaich. 192 pp. Lesbian detective/
disappearing homophobes/upper class gay society.
                                         ISBN 0-941483-25-8   8.95

THE FINER GRAIN by Denise Ohio. 216 pp. Brilliant young
college lesbian novel.   ISBN 0-941483-11-8   8.95

THE AMAZON TRAIL by Lee Lynch. 216 pp. Life, travel & lore
of famous lesbian author.   ISBN 0-941483-27-4   8.95

HIGH CONTRAST by Jessie Lattimore. 264 pp. Women of the
Crystal Palace.   ISBN 0-941483-17-7   8.95

OCTOBER OBSESSION by Meredith More. Josie's rich, secret
Lesbian life.   ISBN 0-941483-18-5   8.95

LESBIAN CROSSROADS by Ruth Baetz. 276 pp. Contemporary
Lesbian lives.   ISBN 0-941483-21-5   9.95

BEFORE STONEWALL: THE MAKING OF A GAY AND
LESBIAN COMMUNITY by Andrea Weiss & Greta Schiller.
96 pp., 25 illus.   ISBN 0-941483-20-7   7.95

WE WALK THE BACK OF THE TIGER by Patricia A. Murphy.
192 pp. Romantic Lesbian novel/beginning women's movement.
                                         ISBN 0-941483-13-4   8.95

SUNDAY'S CHILD by Joyce Bright. 216 pp. Lesbian athletics, at
last the novel about sports.   ISBN 0-941483-12-6   8.95

OSTEN'S BAY by Zenobia N. Vole. 204 pp. Sizzling adventure
romance set on Bonaire.   ISBN 0-941483-15-0   8.95

LESSONS IN MURDER by Claire McNab. 216 pp. 1st Det. Inspec.
Carol Ashton mystery — erotic tension!. ISBN 0-941483-14-2   8.95

YELLOWTHROAT by Penny Hayes. 240 pp. Margarita, bandit,
kidnaps Julia.   ISBN 0-941483-10-X   8.95

SAPPHISTRY: THE BOOK OF LESBIAN SEXUALITY by
Pat Califia. 3d edition, revised. 208 pp.   ISBN 0-941483-24-X   8.95

CHERISHED LOVE by Evelyn Kennedy. 192 pp. Erotic
Lesbian love story.   ISBN 0-941483-08-8   8.95

LAST SEPTEMBER by Helen R. Hull. 208 pp. Six stories & a
glorious novella.   ISBN 0-941483-09-6   8.95

THE SECRET IN THE BIRD by Camarin Grae. 312 pp. Striking,
psychological suspense novel.   ISBN 0-941483-05-3   8.95

TO THE LIGHTNING by Catherine Ennis. 208 pp. Romantic
Lesbian 'Robinson Crusoe' adventure.   ISBN 0-941483-06-1   8.95

THE OTHER SIDE OF VENUS by Shirley Verel. 224 pp.
Luminous, romantic love story.   ISBN 0-941483-07-X   8.95

DREAMS AND SWORDS by Katherine V. Forrest. 192 pp.
Romantic, erotic, imaginative stories.   ISBN 0-941483-03-7   8.95

MEMORY BOARD by Jane Rule. 336 pp. Memorable novel
about an aging Lesbian couple.   ISBN 0-941483-02-9   8.95

THE ALWAYS ANONYMOUS BEAST by Lauren Wright
Douglas. 224 pp. A Caitlin Reese mystery. First in a series.
                                         ISBN 0-941483-04-5   8.95

SEARCHING FOR SPRING by Patricia A. Murphy. 224 pp.
Novel about the recovery of love.   ISBN 0-941483-00-2   8.95

DUSTY'S QUEEN OF HEARTS DINER by Lee Lynch. 240 pp.
Romantic blue-collar novel.　　　　ISBN 0-941483-01-0　　8.95

PARENTS MATTER by Ann Muller. 240 pp. Parents'
relationships with Lesbian daughters and gay sons.
　　　　　　　　　　　　　　　ISBN 0-930044-91-6　　9.95

THE PEARLS by Shelley Smith. 176 pp. Passion and fun in
the Caribbean sun.　　　　　　　ISBN 0-930044-93-2　　7.95

MAGDALENA by Sarah Aldridge. 352 pp. Epic Lesbian novel
set on three continents.　　　　　ISBN 0-930044-99-1　　8.95

THE BLACK AND WHITE OF IT by Ann Allen Shockley.
144 pp. Short stories.　　　　　　ISBN 0-930044-96-7　　7.95

SAY JESUS AND COME TO ME by Ann Allen Shockley. 288
pp. Contemporary romance.　　　　ISBN 0-930044-98-3　　8.95

LOVING HER by Ann Allen Shockley. 192 pp. Romantic love
story.　　　　　　　　　　　　　ISBN 0-930044-97-5　　7.95

MURDER AT THE NIGHTWOOD BAR by Katherine V.
Forrest. 240 pp. A Kate Delafield mystery. Second in a series.
　　　　　　　　　　　　　　　ISBN 0-930044-92-4　　8.95

ZOE'S BOOK by Gail Pass. 224 pp. Passionate, obsessive love
story.　　　　　　　　　　　　　ISBN 0-930044-95-9　　7.95

WINGED DANCER by Camarin Grae. 228 pp. Erotic Lesbian
adventure story.　　　　　　　　ISBN 0-930044-88-6　　8.95

PAZ by Camarin Grae. 336 pp. Romantic Lesbian adventurer
with the power to change the world.　ISBN 0-930044-89-4　　8.95

SOUL SNATCHER by Camarin Grae. 224 pp. A puzzle, an
adventure, a mystery — Lesbian romance.　ISBN 0-930044-90-8　　8.95

THE LOVE OF GOOD WOMEN by Isabel Miller. 224 pp.
Long-awaited new novel by the author of the beloved *Patience
and Sarah.*　　　　　　　　　　ISBN 0-930044-81-9　　8.95

THE HOUSE AT PELHAM FALLS by Brenda Weathers. 240
pp. Suspenseful Lesbian ghost story.　ISBN 0-930044-79-7　　7.95

HOME IN YOUR HANDS by Lee Lynch. 240 pp. More stories
from the author of *Old Dyke Tales.*　ISBN 0-930044-80-0　　7.95

EACH HAND A MAP by Anita Skeen. 112 pp. Real-life poems
that touch us all.　　　　　　　ISBN 0-930044-82-7　　6.95

SURPLUS by Sylvia Stevenson. 342 pp. A classic early Lesbian
novel.　　　　　　　　　　　　ISBN 0-930044-78-9　　7.95

PEMBROKE PARK by Michelle Martin. 256 pp. Derring-do
and daring romance in Regency England.　ISBN 0-930044-77-0　　7.95

THE LONG TRAIL by Penny Hayes. 248 pp. Vivid adventures
of two women in love in the old west.　ISBN 0-930044-76-2　　8.95

HORIZON OF THE HEART by Shelley Smith. 192 pp. Hot
romance in summertime New England.   ISBN 0-930044-75-4   7.95

AN EMERGENCE OF GREEN by Katherine V. Forrest. 288
pp. Powerful novel of sexual discovery.   ISBN 0-930044-69-X   8.95

THE LESBIAN PERIODICALS INDEX edited by Claire
Potter. 432 pp. Author & subject index.   ISBN 0-930044-74-6   29.95

DESERT OF THE HEART by Jane Rule. 224 pp. A classic;
basis for the movie *Desert Hearts*.   ISBN 0-930044-73-8   7.95

SPRING FORWARD/FALL BACK by Sheila Ortiz Taylor.
288 pp. Literary novel of timeless love.   ISBN 0-930044-70-3   7.95

FOR KEEPS by Elisabeth Nonas. 144 pp. Contemporary novel
about losing and finding love.   ISBN 0-930044-71-1   7.95

TORCHLIGHT TO VALHALLA by Gale Wilhelm. 128 pp.
Classic novel by a great Lesbian writer.   ISBN 0-930044-68-1   7.95

LESBIAN NUNS: BREAKING SILENCE edited by Rosemary
Curb and Nancy Manahan. 432 pp. Unprecedented autobiographies
of religious life.   ISBN 0-930044-62-2   9.95

THE SWASHBUCKLER by Lee Lynch. 288 pp. Colorful novel
set in Greenwich Village in the sixties.   ISBN 0-930044-66-5   8.95

MISFORTUNE'S FRIEND by Sarah Aldridge. 320 pp. Histori-
cal Lesbian novel set on two continents.   ISBN 0-930044-67-3   7.95

A STUDIO OF ONE'S OWN by Ann Stokes. Edited by
Dolores Klaich. 128 pp. Autobiography.   ISBN 0-930044-64-9   7.95

SEX VARIANT WOMEN IN LITERATURE by Jeannette
Howard Foster. 448 pp. Literary history.   ISBN 0-930044-65-7   8.95

A HOT-EYED MODERATE by Jane Rule. 252 pp. Hard-hitting
essays on gay life; writing; art.   ISBN 0-930044-57-6   7.95

INLAND PASSAGE AND OTHER STORIES by Jane Rule.
288 pp. Wide-ranging new collection.   ISBN 0-930044-56-8   7.95

WE TOO ARE DRIFTING by Gale Wilhelm. 128 pp. Timeless
Lesbian novel, a masterpiece.   ISBN 0-930044-61-4   6.95

AMATEUR CITY by Katherine V. Forrest. 224 pp. A Kate
Delafield mystery. First in a series.   ISBN 0-930044-55-X   7.95

THE SOPHIE HOROWITZ STORY by Sarah Schulman. 176
pp. Engaging novel of madcap intrigue.   ISBN 0-930044-54-1   7.95

THE BURNTON WIDOWS by Vickie P. McConnell. 272 pp. A
Nyla Wade mystery, second in the series.   ISBN 0-930044-52-5   7.95

OLD DYKE TALES by Lee Lynch. 224 pp. Extraordinary
stories of our diverse Lesbian lives.   ISBN 0-930044-51-7   8.95

DAUGHTERS OF A CORAL DAWN by Katherine V. Forrest.
240 pp. Novel set in a Lesbian new world.   ISBN 0-930044-50-9   7.95

THE PRICE OF SALT by Claire Morgan. 288 pp. A milestone
novel, a beloved classic.   ISBN 0-930044-49-5   8.95

AGAINST THE SEASON by Jane Rule. 224 pp. Luminous,
complex novel of interrelationships.   ISBN 0-930044-48-7   8.95

LOVERS IN THE PRESENT AFTERNOON by Kathleen
Fleming. 288 pp. A novel about recovery and growth.
                                             ISBN 0-930044-46-0   8.95

TOOTHPICK HOUSE by Lee Lynch. 264 pp. Love between
two Lesbians of different classes.   ISBN 0-930044-45-2   7.95

MADAME AURORA by Sarah Aldridge. 256 pp. Historical
novel featuring a charismatic "seer."   ISBN 0-930044-44-4   7.95

CURIOUS WINE by Katherine V. Forrest. 176 pp. Passionate
Lesbian love story, a best-seller.   ISBN 0-930044-43-6   8.95

BLACK LESBIAN IN WHITE AMERICA by Anita Cornwell.
141 pp. Stories, essays, autobiography.   ISBN 0-930044-41-X   7.50

CONTRACT WITH THE WORLD by Jane Rule. 340 pp.
Powerful, panoramic novel of gay life.   ISBN 0-930044-28-2   7.95

YANTRAS OF WOMANLOVE by Tee A. Corinne. 64 pp.
Photos by noted Lesbian photographer.   ISBN 0-930044-30-4   6.95

MRS. PORTER'S LETTER by Vicki P. McConnell. 224 pp.
The first Nyla Wade mystery.   ISBN 0-930044-29-0   7.95

TO THE CLEVELAND STATION by Carol Anne Douglas.
192 pp. Interracial Lesbian love story.   ISBN 0-930044-27-4   6.95

THE NESTING PLACE by Sarah Aldridge. 224 pp. A
three-woman triangle—love conquers all!   ISBN 0-930044-26-6   7.95

THIS IS NOT FOR YOU by Jane Rule. 284 pp. A letter to a
beloved is also an intricate novel.   ISBN 0-930044-25-8   8.95

FAULTLINE by Sheila Ortiz Taylor. 140 pp. Warm, funny,
literate story of a startling family.   ISBN 0-930044-24-X   6.95

THE LESBIAN IN LITERATURE by Barbara Grier. 3d ed.
Foreword by Maida Tilchen. 240 pp. Comprehensive bibliography.
Literary ratings; rare photos.   ISBN 0-930044-23-1   7.95

ANNA'S COUNTRY by Elizabeth Lang. 208 pp. A woman
finds her Lesbian identity.   ISBN 0-930044-19-3   6.95

PRISM by Valerie Taylor. 158 pp. A love affair between two
women in their sixties.   ISBN 0-930044-18-5   6.95

BLACK LESBIANS: AN ANNOTATED BIBLIOGRAPHY
compiled by J. R. Roberts. Foreword by Barbara Smith. 112 pp.
Award-winning bibliography.   ISBN 0-930044-21-5   5.95

THE MARQUISE AND THE NOVICE by Victoria Ramstetter.
108 pp. A Lesbian Gothic novel.   ISBN 0-930044-16-9   4.95

OUTLANDER by Jane Rule. 207 pp. Short stories and essays
by one of our finest writers.   ISBN 0-930044-17-7   8.95

ALL TRUE LOVERS by Sarah Aldridge. 292 pp. Romantic
novel set in the 1930s and 1940s.   ISBN 0-930044-10-X   7.95

A WOMAN APPEARED TO ME by Renee Vivien. 65 pp. A
classic; translated by Jeannette H. Foster.   ISBN 0-930044-06-1   5.00

CYTHEREA'S BREATH by Sarah Aldridge. 240 pp. Romantic
novel about women's entrance into medicine.
                                            ISBN 0-930044-02-9   6.95

TOTTIE by Sarah Aldridge. 181 pp. Lesbian romance in the
turmoil of the sixties.   ISBN 0-930044-01-0   6.95

THE LATECOMER by Sarah Aldridge. 107 pp. A delicate love
story.   ISBN 0-930044-00-2   5.00

ODD GIRL OUT by Ann Bannon.   ISBN 0-930044-83-5   5.95

I AM A WOMAN by Ann Bannon.   ISBN 0-930044-84-3   5.95

WOMEN IN THE SHADOWS by Ann Bannon.
                                            ISBN 0-930044-85-1   5.95

JOURNEY TO A WOMAN by Ann Bannon.
                                            ISBN 0-930044-86-X   5.95

BEEBO BRINKER by Ann Bannon.   ISBN 0-930044-87-8   5.95
     Legendary novels written in the fifties and sixties,
            set in the gay mecca of Greenwich Village.

VOLUTE BOOKS

JOURNEY TO FULFILLMENT   Early classics by Valerie   3.95

A WORLD WITHOUT MEN   Taylor: The Erika Frohmann   3.95

RETURN TO LESBOS   series.   3.95

These are just a few of the many Naiad Press titles — we are the oldest and
largest lesbian/feminist publishing company in the world. Please request a
complete catalog. We offer personal service; we encourage and welcome
direct mail orders from individuals who have limited access to bookstores
carrying our publications.